Psalm 96:3
"Declare to the nations, his marvelous ___ among all the peoples."

Vapors

Paulette L. Harris

a novel by
Paulette Harris

Copyright © 2012 – Paulette Harris
All rights reserved.

ISBN: 1477527389
ISBN-13: 978-1477527382

WHAT PEOPLE SAY ABOUT
Vapors

*"You will not want to put 'VAPORS' down until you've finished it!
Paulette Harris has an intelligent and descriptive writing style that will have you begging for more.
Her writing immediately draws you into the story and the characters lives. You become one of the cast as you read."*

Carolyn Clark
www.TheRoadToAcceptance.com

Vapors is a work of fiction and all characters, incidents, and dialogues are a product of the authors imagination, used fictitiously. Any resemblance to actual persons, living or dead, places or events, is purely coincidental.

Dedicated To -

My dear husband and my family who have supported me through this journey.

Acknowledgements -

Gretchen Ricker, Naphtalie Joiner, Diana Weir, & Jan Verhoeff and numerous friends for their support and assistance in publishing my book. I'm humbly grateful.

Vapors

A novel by Paulette Harris

Original publication by
Full Sail Books
www.FullSailBooks.com

Interior Design by JV Publications
www.JVPublications.com

Cover by Naphtalie Joiner
Scatterjoy Designs

Preface

James 4:14…whereas you do not know what will happen tomorrow, for what is your life? It is even a vapor that appears for a little time and then vanishes away. (NKJV)

Krucshev's voice crawled over the radio waves one year and I'll never forget his menacing tone. He laughed, "You Americans are so afraid with the idea of nuclear bombs and bomb shelters. We'll never bomb you." He promised. "We'll bury you!"

The sneer I heard made me shiver. The Cuban Crises that caused long hours for President Kennedy and people scrambling to build underground shelters was child's play. The man many people around the world feared spat out that the United States of America would cause its own collapse by becoming divided in their culture and belief system. The break-up would start within our own ranks, our beloved families. "America will implode; she'll cause her own destruction." The man gleefully announced.

I often wondered why others didn't seem to talk about it or notice the subtle changes over the years. I felt scared as rumors of wars and wars around me increased. All these recent current events point to a meltdown in our society. Politics and history are intriguing to me and I began to connect the dots. I felt relieved that I wasn't the only vapor that saw a clear warning to life as we know it in the United States.

Who remembers the "Killing Fields"? George Orewells, "1984", The Cuban Crises, C.S. Lewis, and more recently, Bengazi? Do we learn from History…or even know our history?

The only way I can possibly connect the dots from one moment in time in our American History to another and on into the future is to pick up the Bible. That's what my two heroes did, listened and marched. Their meeting at the Wailing Wall only re-enforced what they believed and they moved forward together.

Vapors, just a short dash between the first and last breath we take on earth. A mist that curls around our feet and heads on upward into the firmament, the vapor of life extended. A ray of sun hits the mist and poof! It's gone. That's how suddenly we appear and then disappear. Life's short and there isn't much time left as we know it. If we are lucky we get on the average 80 years, no matter how hard man tries to manipulate his life or others. All the exercise, good food, warm or cool environments, isn't going to make much difference in the scheme of things. None of us wants to be blindsided. Prepared...a soldier doesn't go to war with a dirty gun, it's cleaned and he has his helmet on his head, not in his hand. Are you ready? Do you hear the drum-beat in your life?

Where we are in history could be more truthful and hurt far worse than what we realize. What started out as "American is invincible." to "What in the world is going on here?" is a valid question. The world, as we humans vaporize today, is spinning out of control. To take responsibility and stand up for our freedoms and rights today is scary. Life here will get worse, I guarantee it. The closer we move to the European market, the more you will have to make your own personal decisions about what is best for you and your children. Otherwise, they will be taken and raised in a society that you aren't familiar with and have no control over. I won't lie about what the future holds as I see it.

I finished writing the last pages of Vapors three days before 9/11. It felt like a clock had gone off as events sped up from that moment, kind of a time warp, sci-fi, I can't believe it was true, feelings of dread spread over me. The pressure cooker had finally blown its top as it whistled a loud warning seconds before the potatoes hit the ceiling. "We didn't quite get it when Pearl Harbor blew up, now more warnings, louder, were clearly sounding off to the United States. We truly are not invincible. What was I going to do with this novel? It screamed to be re-edited at every turn of events since that frozen moment in time. These surreal events proved to be facts that point to America's demise.

Who do we trust? What is the truth? What can we do about

it? Why us, supposedly the greatest nation on earth? Where are the answers to a hurting world? Aren't we supposed to help one another? What are boundaries? Which way do we go now??? All these questions beg for answers in a world filled with confusion and terror.

To answer your question, "Why did you write this story?" To be on guard and watch the events unfold around them. Vapors weighs on my heart every day since writing the story. It's an intriguing novel about two average men who are just like you and me. They obeyed a calling to serve the world and its inhabitants. Like atmospheric vapors, they are here for just a short time, warning, inviting, encouraging, crying, and loving us clear to the end of what we embrace. What will we do with the information we have been given? The responsibility is yours to secretly cling to your breast or share with others. There are many valid thoughts going around about who these men are, but only time will tell. Watch for them, perhaps these vapors are already here among us. Or, as the enemy calls them, mosquitoes, are you a mosquito, an annoyance to the world?

I wish to thank all of you, especially my families, who have been involved in encouraging me to move forward with this book.

Chapter 1

She didn't struggle or cry out as gravity claimed her body. Wind and sea roared in her ears, drowning out any noise she could have made.

The moment happened so fast, Susan lost her breath as she slipped on the damp grass near the edge of the cliff. She struggled to get up but as she did, her feet slipped backward and she leaned against the fall. She gasped as she fell to her hands and knees. Full of mud and covered in wet grass, Susan planted one foot in front of her body and pushed herself up with both hands and her good leg.

"David!" Panic-stricken, she cried out. She prayed for a firm stance in the mud with her other foot as she tried to stand straight and balance herself. As she stood up, both feet slipped backward again and she slid over the edge. She grasped empty air as her body hurled downward, catching a protruding cypress branch underneath the overhanging cliff. A blood curdling scream escaped as she pulled at the cypress branch, screaming for David, whom she could no longer see.

David's face appeared above her near the edge of the cliff. He bent down and looked into her eyes as she clung to the withered branch.

"Here Susan, reach for me. I've got you. Don't struggle. Hold on." He was lying on the sod above her, dragging her toward him, but the soft, muddy soil kept giving way above her.

Susan could no longer hold onto the branch and her husband's hands. She lost her grip on the branch. Terrified, she clawed at David's shirt sleeve. She grasped hold, only for her hand to slip away, he let go of her out stretched arms. With horror, she gazed deep into David's eyes, glowing yellow and a red fire near the center.

He growled, "Go home, sweetheart."

He let go and pushed away from her.

Her head connected with a protruding rock three-quarter of the way down the cliff face. She struggled to keep from losing consciousness, but failed.

Earlier in the day, after a rushed breakfast, David and Susan Roberts had driven to Goat Rock State Beach along the Northern California coast. They wanted to catch the sunrise and take photos for the photography class they enrolled in. Dense dark gray fog covered the coast as they got out of their dark blue Lincoln on the cliffs above the beach.

Rough, cold wind smacked Susan. She shivered as she pulled her sweater tighter around her body. "*I wish I would have brought a warmer coat instead.*" She hung her new Canon camera around her neck and leaned across the roof of the car. "Do you need me to grab anything?"

"Grab our jackets and I'll set up the equipment," David pointed to the back seat as he opened the trunk.

Her wind jacket sleeves fought the chilling breezes as she tried to pull them onto her arms. Susan observed the scene, pleased that David had chosen this spot for their assignment.

Nobody could have asked for a better place than Goat Rock, with its rugged, raw beauty.

Susan danced around David and her blue eyes twinkled. She stretched her arms upwards and flung her head back. "I've felt so cooped up the last couple of months."

David wiped his mouth with the back of his hand. "Keep on track and concentrate."

"What did you say? You're *so* bossy,"

David interrupted her sharply, "We don't have all day. Just let me catch this sunrise and then we can walk together. Is that asking too much, Susan?" He pretended to take her picture, adjusting the camera. "Come on, model lady, show me some poses…"

His earlier crankiness suddenly disappeared. *What was he up to? All the way here he was cranky. Now he's being friendly. Oh, well, if he's going to be nicer, I'll enjoy the moment.*

Susan pulled her windblown black hair out of her face and twisted it up with a clip. "There, that's better."

A few people, half a dozen or so, walked along the beach below and a recreational vehicle sat in the designated camping area of the State Park. This location provided a magnificent view of the ocean. A large number of seals barked at the squawking seagulls that took flight over dark angry water in search of a fish breakfast. The morning promised some beautiful shots. Aqua-blue sky showed through the light gray fog rapidly breaking up in the cold morning wind. Spray from the deafening waves exploded toward the top of the cliffs. A final winter storm approached.

Susan pointed her camera at David and grinned. "Hey hunk, I like what I see. You are so handsome and you haven't changed a bit. Well, except for a couple of gray hairs painted in the right places, naturally. You're my own personal Bond Man." She played with her camera, checking different angles of her husband. She liked what she saw.

They enjoyed a good relationship in the beginning.

What happened to make him change so much? He seemed distracted by his job and unpredictable most of the time to the point of rage. Often she was on guard sensing his moods and withdrew when he became difficult to be around.

Incurable lupus devoured her body, fed on stress. Susan had learned this fact well. She sighed and bit her lip. David had no idea of the pressure he put on her. Like most people, he didn't think she looked sick.

Susan's left hip needed to be replaced and they both knew it. She promised David she would have it done in the fall because she wanted to enjoy their first summer together on the West Coast. She tried hard to avoid weakening it any further. If she was cautious, she could make it last a little longer.

Susan was distracted by a man strolling on the beach below her. She noticed the heavy frosty dew on the wild grasses and young blooming ice-plants. The foliage caught sparkles of morning light, looking like they had spent the night in Narnia. Her foot slipped and she caught her breath as she reminded herself to be extra careful. The March wind bit her limbs as she shoved her fingers in the pockets of her jacket and stamped her feet to wake them up.

Suddenly, rays of golden sun light broke through and threads of color spun against the clouds, interweaving the ocean spray and coloring the jutting cliffs. A rainbow formed over Goat Rock.

"Hurry, Susan, before we miss snapping this picture. Go stand over there." David pointed to the edge of the cliff. "Okay step back ... another step or two. I want to get the flowers in the picture."

"I'm afraid to move any closer to the edge, David." Susan hesitated and then moved back.

"Careful, you're crushing the plants." He jerked the camera away from a shooting position.

Chapter 2

Susan woke, as rain slashed at her. She winced in pain as she tried to move her ankle. She knew she had to get out of the rocks. She sensed the tide coming in and the angry sky growing darker.

She struggled with slippery rocks and freed her foot from a low tide pool. Frightened, she jumped back as a small hermit crab slowly made its way up her leg. For a split second she was distracted from her predicament as she picked him up and put him back in the water. Hurt, Susan crawled out. She put her hand on her forehead just before she stood up and fainted.

Late afternoon fog immersed the coast as the cold Pacific water lapped at Susan's body reviving her a second time. She stood up shivering and struggled to understand what happened. Her ankle was numb and her head ached unmercifully. She realized she needed to find warmth and get some dry clothing.

Off in the distance a search and rescue helicopter with large lights flew inland.

She heard nothing but the rushing tides moving in and out against the rocky cliffs. Susan managed to find the road leading back up to the main highway. After what seemed like hours later, she made it to the highway at the top of the hill. She saw headlights up the road. Wet and cold, Susan sank down on the wet night sand and tried to see her watch. "Thank goodness the little light wasn't broken." The injured woman began mumbling to herself. "The time says 10:35 PM. Now what am I going to do?"

She kept moving.

Her thoughts drifting to the horror she felt as David let her go. "I can't think about that right now." Susan pushed ugly uprising thoughts further down into her mind, way beyond past her gut feelings.

"Oh, look at the lights ahead! Please somebody let these people open the door and help me!" She cried out loud. Light poured from the windows of the little grey cottage and smoke blew from the chimney as the wind and rain increased their intensity.

***

"Molly, come quick," Doctor Randall called out to his wife as he opened the door. "I think this is the lady on the news; the one that the air and sea rescue has been looking for all day."

Molly brought dry towels and after rubbing Susan down, got her into the bathroom where she laid out some soft flannel pajamas, a fluffy robe, and slipper socks.

"What do you think honey?" She anxiously queried as her orthopedic husband's expert hands moved up and down Susan's left ankle.

"Well, at least I don't think it's broken," He assured the two ladies. "You're very lucky indeed, but we should call the authorities as soon as you are rested. An x-ray wouldn't hurt at this point either."

"No, don't call anyone; I just want some aspirin and hot cup of coffee for this awful headache." Susan begged while Randall looked at her head and found an angry bump in her hairline. There were no cuts so he felt this area would be all right as well.

Molly brought three full steaming mugs of coffee along with some toast on a colorful mosaic tray. In between tears, Susan managed to tell Randall and Molly the events of that day. Molly patted her on the leg and spoke, "It's time that we should go to bed now Susan and we'll decide what to do tomorrow. In the meantime, I've made up the sofa for you in front of the warm fire." She smiled. "You're welcome and safe here in our home. It's a wonder that Randall and I decided to get away this weekend. The next closest house is a quarter of a mile further up the road. Goodnight." She gave Susan a hug.

"And, get rest. Those are doctor's orders," Randall grinned.

Susan curled up under the clean sheets and stared into the flickering flames. The storm was roaring outside, but inside it was a quiet comforting haven of safety.

How many times had she thought to herself, *Enough for one day*? She drifted off to sleep meaning every word.

She slept fitfully and dreamed of sea-gulls screaming at her with a full moon that tugged her down somewhere she didn't want to go. She jumped up at three in the morning. Sweat ran down her face and neck as she turned to look at the clock. Lying in the faint light of glowing embers, she realized she must face the truth. Maybe Randall could help with some direction. There were too many problems over the years between David and her. Every time an incident would happen, he would cry and plead for her forgiveness. Susan thought that this move out west, an entirely different environment would change him. She shrugged; she knew better. Deep inside she knew no one changes unless they want to. David couldn't face the fact that he carried problems and needed help. Most of the time it was her fault, he told her. She made him do things he didn't like. He didn't want to be mean to her, but she just drove him to it. She could be so difficult to get along with, according to David. Tears rolled down her cheeks. The biggest problem was she didn't know what she was doing wrong to set him off.

    His tantrums had become more frequent. At thirty five, she was sorry she was so ill and couldn't get better. After a long sigh and a thought that perhaps things would be clearer in the morning, she fell asleep; this time soundly.

    The storm raged for three days, and at Susan's request Randall and Molly allowed her to stay with them. The phone lines were down.

Chapter 3

High on the roof top balcony at the University of San Francisco Hospital, Molly and Susan breathed in the fresh clean air. A bright sun was shining and the air was balmy. Molly questioned her new friend as she offered her coffee and commented about the beautiful day. The weather was certainly a contrast to the past couple of weeks. Randall would be joining them after his last patient.

As he approached them with a copy of Susan's x-rays of her ankle, he smiled, "Great news!" Randall reached to give his wife a hug and pecked her cheek. "Susan's ankle is just fine."

"Thanks Randall, how can I ever repay you?" He laughed when he heard Susan ask and told her he wrote the favor off.

"Someone owed me," he responded and that was that. He inquired as to how things played out. The Search and Rescue Team had been called off and to the world; Susan was officially lost at sea. It was presumed that she'd been swept out and became caught in the undertow after she fell into the icy Pacific waters. She was for all intents purposes dead. The police, sheriff, and Detective Lane made sure of the finality.

Detective Lane arrived to drive her to the police station for more statements and as she rode in the unidentified car, Susan thought to herself how strange it was, a few days earlier, that she was reading about her own memorial service. No family, no friends in attendance; just David throwing a huge wreath of her favorite flowers, yellow and white jonquils and daffodils into the foaming waves below.

***

Grim faced, Detective Lane offered Susan a chair and cup of coffee as she entered his office. She was apprehensive as she accepted it, noticing three somber men in suits already seated. Detective Lane, a professional in his world was a perfectionist too. He cleared his throat for full attention from the four people seated in front of him. "I'm coming straight to the point Susan. These three gentlemen are FBI Agents and you are ordered under their care as of right now."

"But…" Susan began.

"You are to trust no one and you will be informed on a need to know basis." He interrupted. "The boys here have been caught up to date on this case, and I'm going to let them fill you in. This is bigger than you can imagine and we are going to need your help. For the time being we will give you a new identity and put you under protective custody."

"Where will I be?" Susan asked.

"Your sister in Seattle will need you to visit. You, of course, won't really be at your sister's home."

"What about my sister Jan and her husband; you are going to protect them too, right?" One of the agents spoke up. "Yes ma'am; they've already been briefed."

Susan panicked as she began to realize how extensive this investigation was becoming. "What do I tell Molly and Randall?"

"Same thing," the agent replied.

Detective Lane interrupted, "We're getting ahead of ourselves. How about bringing her up to date and then maybe things will make more sense."

Agent One spoke up, "Susan what do you really know about your husband?"

She replied, "I thought I knew everything. Goodness! We've been married almost fifteen years! I met him in San Francisco where he was on assignment for some of the war demonstrations and marches around the San Francisco Bay area. During that time I was going to Stanford, studying engineering, hoping to get into a start-up company in Silicon Valley when I graduated. David was dating my roommate whenever he came to town. Nothing was serious though for either of them. I knew he was a war correspondent during the Vietnam War. He came back from that assignment a very angry man. David worked for the same newspaper and television broadcasting company forever. My roommate stood him up one night, I was available and the rest is history." Susan smiled as she re-called the past. "I was smitten. He has the most beautiful piercing blue eyes. Another very important plus about him was that he is taller than me. I am tall and modeled for college money. Our romance was a whirlwind." She shrugged her shoulders. "I guess a lot of them were with the war going on. We saw each other every day for three or four months."

"He flew back to New York and I was involved with my classes. He called often and then one night was different. He was agitated and said he volunteered to go to Vietnam, even though he had been passed over because of his college studies. He told me that he needed this experience to put together the final touch to some of the pieces he was working on. I was sorry to see him go but I wasn't into this war at all. I never understood the whole mess and I'm ashamed to admit, I didn't care." She rolled her eyes and added, "Unlike most of my peers, who were out debating and protesting much of the time? Well, it just seemed that they were making way too much out of it. My father, grandfather, and great-grandfather were all war heroes. They did what their country called them to do. I don't understand why they couldn't just let our soldiers do their duty?" Susan paused after a long sigh, and then continued. "I remember that David used to get so upset with me for lack of concern or the need to know. I didn't hear from him for a month. One night he called and told me he was in the city and wanted to come over. I remember it was on a Friday and spring-break was coming up."

Susan pulled her hair out of her face and pushed it back with a clip, "I just finished my final exams, did well, and in the mood to celebrate. We spent the whole week together, every moment. That week I realized, I loved him. He was quick and funny. David's spontaneity was what attracted me. I can be so focused, I'm boring!" Susan laughed out loud and for a few moments everyone in the somber office smiled.

One of the agents looked at his watch and said, "I think it's time for a break."

They sent out for Chinese and after lunch Susan continued. "Well, we ended up getting married in Nevada and as the saying goes, never looked back. David returned to Vietnam; by then he told me the war was wrapping up and soon our troops would be coming home. I kept busy during that summer of 1972 working at a couple of different companies in San Jose, California." Susan sighed, "They were involved with chemicals, processing, computers, research and development."

"Dad and Mom were upset about the quick marriage but they loved David and were proud of our independence. He was such a handsome gentleman, everyone loved him. They were involved with my sisters' new baby boy and so all was going well."

"David came home that fall and we moved to New York City. Our life was full. The world of news is fascinating and I worked at being the best wife I could be. David didn't want me to work. He all of a sudden wanted children. Three miscarriages later, the doctor insisted on no more tries. We were successful. We enjoyed a nice house and a second beautiful place near Lake

Placid. I learned golf and skiing. David was very athletic and loved competition. He was annoyed because I wouldn't join some of the ladies groups and compete."

"The truth is I am not very athletic. What came easy for him was extra practice and work for me. I was okay, I mean, I could play well enough but competition wasn't enjoyable." Susan shrugged her shoulders and rolled her eyes. "He could drink and party all night. I would have one wine cooler and fall asleep." She shook her head. "I never did understand how he could hop out of bed the next morning with no evidence of drugs and alcohol from the night before. Yes, he could get just about any type of drugs anytime he wished. We argued some about it, but everyone in our social life was into them. Certain types of drugs helped the creative process at least that is what our writer and artist friends used to say. Even the doctors in our circles were into them." Susan shrugged her shoulders again, "I never questioned where they got the stuff."

The distraught woman twisted a strand of black hair. "I began to get sick and the doctors couldn't find the problem. Several surgeries later including a hip-replacement, they figured it was lupus. The disease progressed rapidly and all the medications were taking their toll in other areas. I went into a selected study offered by one of the medical schools and found that my problems were related to chemical exposure. The only thing that the doctors could come up with was the time when I worked in San Jose. Several cases began turning up all of a sudden. We have found the same chemicals from the same areas of the country."

Susan wrung her hands and glanced downward, "David was very good to me through all of this. He began to change though; I could see how impatient he was with everyone and everything around us. It was as if he couldn't control my illness. He told me work wasn't fulfilling any longer and he felt life was passing him by. I figured it was some sort of mid-life crises and a change would help. We decided to move back to California."

Susan re-adjusted her position in the office chair and sighed.

"The climate was easier on my replaced right hip, and we could still go up to Squaw Valley for our snow sports. David loves being in the center of an exciting news life, but he also has the yearning to strike out on his own and do a small paper; maybe as combination of reporter, editor, publisher somewhere along the Pacific Northwest Coast. I wanted to believe he could settle down here but, he didn't. We've only been back a year or so, but he goes to New York once or twice a month. He tells me that he has been wrapping things up. Frankly, I can't imagine what. The house has sold as well as the transfer of our timeshare, and our mountain home is rented. Most of our assets are here with us." She toyed with a torn fingernail.

"He stays with his sister and brother-in-law, who purchased his share of the family home. Whenever I call they are away and don't call back. Most of the time he's gone two or three days so I haven't worried. That is until now. I guess I've buried my head in the sand a little too long, huh guys?" Susan hung her head. "I can't think of much else except recently, he has been quieter and rather secretive. He tells me he will answer the phone when it rings and he has been getting more calls at odd hours. He tells me that they are just calls from New York and the realtors. I believed that he was protecting me from getting overtired. The doctors have advised me to go slow even though I'm feeling better."

"What have you found out?" Susan raised her eyebrow.

***

Agent One began to explain, "We've been watching your husband for the past thirty years."

Susan gasped, "What for?"

Agent Three, who had been silent all morning, answered calmly, "At first, Susan, it was drug trafficking, but after Vietnam new things have begun to surface in his file. He is involved in chemical warfare at the international level. We aren't sure what part he is playing yet. We were beginning to close in, when your presumed death couldn't have been timelier. We can get more information and much further in this case now that we have your help."

"It's ironic, isn't it," Agent Two half-smiled. "You'll be doing your country a good service."

Susan started shaking. "I can't believe this. What could I possibly do?"

Agent Two replied, "For one thing, you can get into your house and help us retrieve some vital information. David will probably let his guard down now that you aren't around."

Agent One was clearly the lead in this operation. He interrupted quite a lot in their conversation and clarified details. He emphasized the seriousness of the situation and told her to trust no one including Molly and Randall. Susan leaned forward and asked for a good reason; after all, they saved her.

Detective Lane touched her arm and glanced at the agents. "I'll tell her." He spoke softly. "Your home has been bugged and wires tapped for some time. There have been a couple of conversations between the good Doctor and David. We don't think it's much yet. Randall wants to do what he thinks is right, helping a grieving husband. He has recommended a couple of doctors of psychiatry for David to talk with in getting help. I don't believe Molly is aware of what he has done."

"What?" Susan cried. "I can't believe what you are telling me! I told you all...David dropped me off those cliffs; he let me go and fall. He told me to let go. He held me by my armpits, he could have pulled me up and he didn't," By now Susan wiped uncontrollable tears that were pouring down her face. "I'm afraid, no, scared to death," she stammered. "What am I going to do?" The hysterical woman sobbed harder.

She stood up and stumbled into Detective Lanes' arms. He held her tight and patted her back like a child and then moving her at arm's length, he pushed her long black hair out of her face.

Chapter 4

Susan fell asleep as soon as the dinner flight to Seattle took off. She had taken a prescription for pain and stress. She lived long enough with the lupus to realize she needed to somehow control the stress that was beginning to create a flare up. The disease had been in remission when they left New York City. Recently, she noticed she began aching all over again and she was not resting well. She decided to seek a rheumatologist and have more blood work done in Seattle. Maybe Jan could help her find one. Thank-goodness she could get hold of some of her assets before they were frozen. The Detective helped her with that and her husband was none the wiser. Agent One was three rows behind. His head was buried in a newspaper and as the plane took flight, he yawned and pretended to fall asleep. He managed to throw in a snore or two for good measure but the team knew full well that he was alert to everyone around them the entire trip.

Jan wanted to be at the airport to meet Susan, but was discouraged. Susan and Agent One took a taxi to her home instead. The two sisters grabbed one another at the front door and petite, blond Jan started to sob. Susan comforted her and while the three drank coffee and ate apple cinnamon cake, the agent explained what would happen next.

"Jan, where is your husband?" Susan asked.

"Ray is overseas working on a big contract," Jan picked up the dishes from the kitchen counter and began loading the dishwasher. "He'll be gone a week."

Agent One spoke up. "It's okay Susan, Jan and Ray received briefings. The less they know the better for everyone. You'll be taken out of town to an undisclosed place, but I know you need to be under a doctor's care so we've found a good one. He's here in Seattle so we can arrange for you to see Jan once in awhile."

Jan began to cry. "Oh Susan, I'm so glad you are alive. It's been hell for us. I can't begin to imagine what it's been like for you."

"Now I understand why no one came for the services David held." Susan shook her head speaking softly. "You're right, it's been hell and my body is screaming at me to give it more rest; so if you don't mind, I'm going to turn in for the night. We can get through this; just by taking one day at a time."

Susan slept well into the next morning, so they stayed with Jan the following night. The sisters enjoyed a relaxing day and spent time cooking and going through pictures. Their parents had passed away a couple of years back. Jan and Susan only had each other so parting was hard. Jan insisted on sending homemade cookies and a Washington apple pie. "You need to be fattened up." She spoke while she packed a lunch basket for the two travelers.

Susan laughed, "You should have seen me two years ago on the prednisone. I looked like a beached baby whale! David used to tell me when my chest stuck out further than my stomach, I would be doing well!" Her smile faded as she remembered a good thing about her husband. She would miss the good things about him. He had a way of taking her worst blue days and helping her turn them around. She gulped down a silent sob and turned to pick her coffee cup from the kitchen counter hiding the tears spilling from her eyes.

Agent One glanced down and pointed at his watch. Jan and Susan hugged. It seemed scary to both for Susan to embark on such a new way of life.

"Where are we going?" Susan questioned the quiet driver. They were heading north. The fog kept her feeling as if they were traveling under cover. She felt like they were the only two people in the world.

Agent One answered, "We are going into Canada. There is a little town along the coast just a ways into the mountains, quiet and isolated. We have a female agent already there that has set up housekeeping. She is a teacher and you are to be her new roommate. Of course there will be talk, it's a small town, but you know in your heart who and what you are. I'll be back and forth to keep you informed."

"Why go into Canada, instead of staying in the States and going inland? It seems to me that some place like Spokane or some smaller place in the Cascades or Rockies would be more suitable...." Susan raised an eyebrow and re-folded the map.

"There are a couple of good reasons, but one of them is that going to Spokane means an Air Force Base nearby. That's not a good thing," Agent One frowned. "David is involved internationally and politically. There could be someone who knows you. You can be sure that David may be looking in Washington for you if he somehow learns that you are still alive. For that one reason, Seattle is out of the question. Besides that, the climate is better for you along the coast."

Susan was surprised. "How do you know?"

Agent One smiled, "I did my homework Susan."

The old white Ford Galaxy purred and soon Susan fell asleep. Agent One reached over and adjusted her pillow and turned the heater on. The sky was dark and cloudy. More fog was moving in as they drove up the coast.

The sun was setting over the Pacific Ocean when the couple pulled up a long driveway lined with evergreen trees. There, nestled among the trees was an inviting log cabin. The front yard was full of shade plants, all in bloom. Despite its smallness, the place looked homey and welcoming.

Susan stepped through an open door and she smelled fresh bread and saw a burning fireplace. Agent Brooke called out in a cheery welcome and threw her arms around Susan. "Come on in! You two must be hungry." Susan realized the fresh air increased her appetite. Agent One and she polished off the sandwiches and cookies they carried with them hours ago. Brooke was excited about the apple pie that Susan brought. She said it complemented the elk stew. Susan wrinkled her nose and tried a taste, relieved that it was good if not better than beef.

Brooke was as talkative as Agent One was quiet. Susan finally asked him his name and he just smiled. "Agent Number One is my name for all intents and purposes Susan. As a matter of fact, Brooke here isn't Brooke either. Let's see Brooke, he looked at her directly, but with twinkling eyes, what is your number? Oh yes, it's Agent 57 I believe," he laughed.

"Yes sir! Agent 57 is reporting for duty!" Brooke giggled. By then Susan joined in the joke and laughed with them.

Brooke completed a lot of preparation for their stay before they arrived. The first thing they needed to do was a make-over on Susan. Agent One packed all the necessary paperwork, social security, birth certificate, and drivers' license. Although the three new friends turned in early, Susan couldn't fall asleep. She tried because she was tired, but every time she closed her eyes, she thought of something different. The muscles in her legs twitched and her joints ached, but she noticed that she was breathing much better. Susan tossed and turned, before falling asleep.

"It's shearing time," Brooke chuckled as she picked up the scissors after breakfast.

"I was afraid you'd think of that," Susan frowned.

"Well honey, I hate to be the bad guy, but I'd thought of a cute idea." Brooke babbled away as she worked on Susan's hair. "Your hair is beautiful; the kind I always wanted." The tiny woman sported a round face with fine features. Her hair was cut in a short wedge. With her curly red hair and hazel-green eyes, she was striking. "Oh Susan, you are going to like this," Brooke exclaimed gleefully.

Susan was apprehensive, "I don't know. My hair is so drastically different now. I didn't even lose this much after all the chemotherapy the doctors made me take over five years ago." Long black hair was all over the floor. "Why can't I wear a wig?" Susan whined.

"Because your hair would be too thick underneath one and you'd have trouble keeping it on. Now behave!" Brooke giggled. "Let's do the next step a permanent and golden blond color."

"What!" Susan exclaimed. By the time Brooke was done, it was three in the afternoon. Susan decided she could live with the change. Her new hairdo looked cute. The neck length bob was attractive on her and she liked the wash and wear coils the perm had given her. She shook her head, enjoying the freedom of the lighter weight. Brooke thinned and bleached Susan's brows and taught her to apply color changing makeup that wouldn't look overdone, until she could get used to the look. Susan didn't wear much because of the chemicals in most cosmetics, but Brooke purchased some special types. She did a good job. Agent One added a comment. His futuristic cell phone occupied him most of the day. The last thing he needed to do was to take a picture and apply it to Susan's new driver's license.

"Viola! A toast to you Susan and to what good things the future will bring." Agent One spoke as they enjoyed an after dinner drink before turning in for the night. "Brooke will fill you in as to the next steps you will take tomorrow, Susan. You are a brave girl." Susan attempted to smile and went to bed. She heard them talking late but couldn't make out the conversation. That night she dreamed of chopping, sawing, cutting, all in the name of new hairdos and wood splitting in the woods.

Agent One was gone before the break of day. Susan woke to the smell of coffee. Light poured through the windows, creating patterns on the floors as she stumbled out from the bathroom. She yawned and stretched, and asked where Agent One was. "Oh, he left early this morning," Brooke answered as if this was a common occurrence. It was in such a way that Susan felt she further questions were unnecessary.

Chapter 5

David, shaken from the events on the cliffs, found it difficult to remember if he'd called anyone for help after Susan's fall. He found himself in a dark bathroom under a running shower. He felt the fog begin to lift as he asked himself over and over what happened.

Suddenly, he felt tired and depressed. Weary of the self inflicted worry, he sipped at a cold brew hoping to diminish the situation. Much later, he dragged himself to bed and fell asleep recalling the events of the early years of his life with Susan and their marriage.

***

David fell to his knees, arms raised above his head, apologizing and pleading for forgiveness. A camouflaged soldier whirled around ready to shoot as David snapped a twig in the remote jungle of Vietnam. "You sorry son-of-a-gun," the soldier grumbled. "I almost blew your head off. What if that stick had been a land mine?" Before David could speak, the man adjusted his M-16 weapon and questioned him further. "What the heck are you doing and how did you get clear out here?"

David squeezed his eyes shut and replied that he had been following their small troop all morning. He explained that he was a war correspondent from the United States. The soldier noticed the camera around David's neck and demanded some identification. Although David tried to dress for the occasion, he realized he was pretty conspicuous compared to his fellow humans. The five soldiers that surrounded him were heavily camouflaged from their heads to their feet. They were hard to spot except for the whites of their eyes. The apparent leader whispered to his four comrades to stop and they carefully stepped back to the waiting man.

"You've put this darn recon patrol in jeopardy, you idiot." The lead soldier added in a harsh hushed tone, "We're too far out to return him. So, we're going to have to hide this jerk and come back for him tonight."

The soldiers dug a hole, and after laying David in it, they covered everything around him with native foliage. "I don't care if you soil yourself; don't you move one inch until we come back for you," ordered the Officer in charge. The men spread out around the area, making sure the enemy wasn't observing their movements. Satisfied, they rendezvoused and continued on their journey.

Until this point, David enjoyed the excitement that his job offered. This day though, would be tattooed in his mind forever. He couldn't remember the last time he'd been so scared. Sometime after darkness fell, he began to wonder if the troop would come back and rescue him, or if they would remember where he was planted. He tried to re-call some of the prayers he was taught as a small boy. Every little sound frightened him, exhaustion settled into his weary bones and each time he drifted off to sleep, something would startle him. He heard strange languages in the area earlier in the afternoon. The humans passed so close, he tried to find his camera and then remembered that it had been confiscated. He held his breath so long; he thought he might pass out.

Hours later, someone shook him awake and jerked him up. "NO TALKING!" ordered a voice in his ear. David was so startled, he obeyed without hesitation. David's feet were sore and several unnamed insect bites demanded to be itched. He hobbled and jumped along scratching at the sores. He was one wet, miserable reporter as the sun came up and he staggered into the army outpost. He was immediately taken to the Base Commander with a full report from the patrol that brought him in. The huge man's demeanor scared David into complete respect.

Commander Planter excused the men and brought David hot coffee. "You look like eight miles of bad road son. What happened?" he drawled in a deep southern accent. The two men conversed for some time and David asked for his camera back. "Tell you what, boy, my

Sergeant here has clean clothes, a hot shower, and breakfast for you, and then we will continue our conversation. Then, you can get some rest."

"Well how do you feel now?" Commander Planter queried as David gulped down his food.

"Much better now; thank you Sir," David gave him a nod.

The Commander returned the unloaded camera to him.

"We destroyed the film," the Commander added in anticipation of an argument. "You put my boys out there and this company in a great deal of danger. The enemy could have known by your photographs the exact location of where they were working. You see this group of men does our mapping and planning along the Cambodian border. We aren't supposed to be running in and out of there. I shouldn't even be giving you this information. By the way, you were supposed to be on our departure plane day before yesterday. What did you do to get yourself in such a mess?"

David explained he slipped out of the cargo door right after everyone boarded the plane and headed straight for the latrines. He started following the small party at about six in the morning. He noticed that they were together and on some sort of mission. He had a couple of candy bars and a soda so thought he could follow till noon or so, and then back track with several rolls of film spent. That was, after all, his job. David wiped his palms on his pant legs as he tried to justify his actions to Captain Planter. He added that his plan was working well until he made the mistake of stepping on that one small stick.

"You people got no sense at all." Commander Planter was shaking his head and frowning. "You will get on the plane this afternoon with no film for your useless camera. You have to realize this is a real war, not war games. Tell that to your people back home, job or no job. Let's get a reality check. We can't do our work if you are going to spill the beans to the enemy in the name of "right to know news." David could tell that this guy meant business and he better not push him. At precisely 1300 hours, military time, David was not only escorted off the base into a cargo plane, but ordered to return to the United States as well.

Chapter 6

San Francisco Airport was full of people, many returning soldiers and their families, huddled in the comfort of family warmth. The hour was late and cold rain came down in torrents.

David thought of giving Susan a call. He changed his mind as he remembered she was deeply involved in her studies. He opted for a dry airport hotel room. A morning call would be better. He also planned to call his boss in New York. Although the room was clean, warm, and comfortable, David tossed and turned all night. He was in and out of foxholes. There were mines exploding around. Next, he was tied up and couldn't get away. He wore camouflaged clothing but the enemy kept taking them off him, one piece at a time. He woke up wrestling with a Viet-cong soldier demanding that he get his clothing and camera back.

David got into the shower and scrubbed until his body was raw, as if to get some of the ugly memories off. He ordered room service and began to shave. Breakfast came with a knock shortly thereafter. David was finishing his last cup of coffee and morning paper when he decided to call the office.

He explained what was happening to his superior. "Boy, David; you have been through the ringer. Tell you what; I know you've got a girl on the West Coast. Stay out there for a week or so and get some rest. If you want to keep working on this assignment, check out what is going on in the public eye. Find out what the public is thinking about how the war is supposed to be progressing. Listen to what they are, thinking, feeling, and saying."

"Yeah that's sound good," David frowned. "There were uniformed soldiers at the airport last night, and there were a lot of people cat calling them as they milled about. There was a segment of disgruntled people hanging out there for sure, some were even picketing. I saw some soldiers being spit upon as they got off the planes. I thought there would be a fight, but the servicemen and women just looked too tired and haggard. Some were terribly thin. The only people I saw smiling were their children."

The next call David made was to Susan. They spoke briefly. She had a final test late in the afternoon and then would be free until the following Monday. They could meet on the condition that she would return early Sunday afternoon to her studies. That evening, when David picked up Susan, he realized for the first time that he missed her. She looked attractive with her waist long black hair and aqua-blue eyes. Her eyes were unusually piercing that evening. David felt as if he were on some exotic island every time he looked at her. He tried to shake off the thought of falling in love with her. No time for this kind of feeling, he kept reminding himself. He was working on a career.

They spent Saturday walking through Golden Gate Park and talking. After lunch at a nearby delicatessen, the two rested lazily; warm sunshine broke through and burned off remaining morning fog. They strolled along Fisherman's Wharf before having dinner. David laughed as they watched the seals play and fight with the seagulls for fish. David ordered a white Napa Valley wine to go with the fresh catch of the day and their meal ended before they realized the sun set.

David moaned as he kissed Susan goodnight on her doorstep. "Please Susan; let me come in for coffee. I need you." He held her tightly in his arms and buried his face in her long hair.

"You excite me and I want to be with you a little longer."

Susan kissed him back long and passionately. "You know how I feel David. I'm very attracted to you but...I'm not ready. No, you can't come in. Mostly because I mean, never mind. You can't come in. I'll see you tomorrow." Susan mumbled. "Okay?"

David frowned and then agreed to pick up Susan early the next day. The plan included a trip to Santa Cruz and then Susan would fix dinner for the both of them. The day went fast as they headed southwest through Pacifica and then down Highway one. Returning north up highway seventeen after a good sunburn and a flat tire, they agreed the day was exhilarating. Dinner was a simple meal with pasta, salad, and San Francisco sourdough bread. A dark zinfandel wine complemented the meal.

The two shared many thoughts and dreams.

"What are your plans now Susan?" asked David.

Susan shrugged her shoulders. "Well I've accepted a position in San Jose, California. It's a new company. I'll be working with tests and instruments in the semi-conductor business. It is the up and coming technology for the future. I suspect there will be a lot of chemical processes as well. I'll be starting work in a couple of weeks."

David leaned back in his chair and clasped his hands behind his head. "I've got some unfinished business overseas. I need to wrap up this war. I've been in touch with my boss every day. He feels it would be good for my career to complete the whole scenario myself."

"Do you really believe it's going to end David?" Susan was, as usual in the dark about the situation. It made David feel good to be able to have important knowledge about the world around him; but it also annoyed him that she was so indifferent to politics and war. He wondered for being so intelligent, why wasn't she more up to date?

***

David looked at her strong innocent face glowing in the candlelight. She was intensely sexual at the moment and he took her face in his hands. "Susan, I'm going to miss you, will you wait for me?" He kissed her neck and trailed along the pulse in her neck to her lips.

She kissed him back and responded to every move. "Oh David, I'm going to miss you as well." David became more demanding. By the time she pushed him away, they were both panting. "David you're going overseas again. I'm here, you're there, and I'm starting a career. I can't promise you anything but for the record, you excite me too," she giggled. "Now get out of here before I get into trouble." She dragged him to the door and pushed him out.

"Are you still going to have dinner with me tomorrow night?" David whined.

Susan laughed, "Of course silly and what would you like me to wear Sir?" David told her about a fine restaurant and they agreed to an early dinner. He reminded her to dress in something special because there would be a band and he wanted to dance into the night.

David realized as he drove back to his hotel that this woman must be all his. He was smitten and he also realized that it would not be long before she gave herself to someone. Her kisses were full of desire. The very thought of her made him squirm.

Chapter 7

Susan eagerly opened the door. She anticipated seeing David. He told her they were going to dinner and dancing afterwards. David handed her a bouquet of red roses and hugged her. He teased her with a lingering kiss. When he stepped back holding her shoulders, he pushed her at arm's length. "You look great Susan." She wore a blue knee length chiffon dress that flowed from the waist down. The deep blue matched her eyes. The sparkling solitaire diamond necklace and earrings were simple, modern designs. Her long black hair was pulled up with a silver barrette and her matching pumps raised her to David's eye level. Together they made a striking couple.

During desert, David grabbed Susan's hand. "Susan will you marry me?" he asked her as he presented her with a blue velvet box.

"Oh David, it is breathtaking." She admired the one karat solitaire emerald cut diamond and said, "Won't you please slip it on my finger? I would love to marry you! I love you David." She kissed him and whispered in his ear.

They danced late into the night and spent the rest of the weekend talking and planning their future together. Susan prepared dinner on Sunday because David had to return to Washington D.C. early Monday morning. He promised her he would return in a month. They planned to marry during Spring Break because Susan would be graduating in June. David had a three month overseas assignment and Susan wanted to work at least until Christmas. They talked for hours about family and where they wanted to live. Each had different ideas, but realized the decisions didn't all have to be made before the wedding. They'd have plenty of time to decide where to live, and when to have a family after they finished their current dreams. Most of the decisions indicated that they would start out, after David returned from his work overseas, and live on the east coast.

***

Two weeks later, Susan answered a knock on her apartment door. To her surprise, David stood there, dripping wet with a bundle of wilted red roses. He said, "I can't wait Susan, please come with me. Let's go to Tahoe and get married tonight?"

"Oh David," she pulled him inside and kissed him. "What a surprise! I have missed you. I could come up with a thousand excuses why not, but...oh well. That's one of the reasons why I love you so much!"

"Good! Now that it is settled, I'll pick you up at six tomorrow morning so we have an early start," he grinned. He gave her a big kiss and playful slap on the arm. "Now get to bed and rest. See you in the morning." Susan waved him out the door. Susan laughed as she threw things in her suitcase, so much for any planning. The only thing she purchased so far was her negligee.

As promised, David arrived early. He opened the car door for Susan and flipped the windshield wipers on to wash the syrupy cold damp fog off the windshield as they pulled out of the city. By the time they reached Sacramento, California, the sun shone brightly and the air was clear. David took out a list, "Check one, check two..." he continued to check off his list and grinned. Pleased that he had everything planned in anticipation so that Susan would agree to the wedding now. Every detail was taken care of, Susan's parents and sister and brother-in-law were there. Her mother presented Susan with a special heirloom wedding dress and everyone enjoyed the small but love-filled wedding.

David never felt more fulfilled or proud than he felt that weekend. Susan was all and more than he ever wanted in a woman. The week was full of lovemaking and planning for the future. They both wanted two children and a dog to go with Susan's calico kitty.

Chapter 8

David wasn't close to his relatives back East. His parents were older when he was born. They died in an auto accident when he was three years old and elderly grandparents raised him. A well liked student, he worked hard and received good grades. He didn't play sports until college where he learned to love competition. He was raised in a small quietly conservative Catholic church. Confused, David wasn't sure what he believed in, especially when it came to the progressive, freedom-loving movement and the Vietnam War. His passion for writing got him a scholarship into a well known Eastern University. His excellent grades and personality helped him break into the news media before he even graduated.

David's eagerness to please several of his bosses sometimes conflicted with his ideas of good reporting. He struggled hard with morals and values. Ethics had always been an issue for him, now they challenged him.

"We don't want your opinions David," they would tell him. "Just report the facts. The editors will put the finishing touches on the final product." He noticed that many of their views tended to be slanted in one direction or another. They weren't altogether truthful in the young reporter's eyes. He began to conform to their requests as time went on.

Often, he and his news crew would get together at each others' houses or for a skiing or golfing weekend trip. By the time they were off the slopes and partying after dinner, a subject would be tossed in the air and an article would be written. David wondered how much the drugs and alcohol influenced a particular piece of work. They spent long hours arguing about Vietnam. Many young men his age were fleeing to San Francisco and Canada to get lost in the crowd and avoid going off to war. Many burned the American Flag and their draft cards. David was exempt because he earned a scholarship to college and he was the sole survivor of his name. Guilt began to gnaw at his being.

***

David returned home and although Susan noticed a more aggressive man, she believed it was because of his career. They built a home together and every weekend was filled with some sport or social event. Often they could be found at Lake Placid, New York or San Francisco to visit her family who adored David. Life was exciting and busy.

Returning from reporting in Vietnam a second time, David didn't allow himself to see the anger that was stuffed inside. He kept busy reporting and keeping his own home life happy. Susan was great at being a help-mate and home-maker. She could be fun at parties but she could also be a bore. He would try to include her in their conversations but she wasn't interested in "news-talk" as she called it. She would rather drag one of the wives into the kitchen or discuss children.

David desperately wanted children but Susan experienced trouble carrying babies and after three miscarriages, the doctor suggested she have her tubes tied. That put a strain on the marriage as well as many arguments about drugs and alcohol.

Susan tolerated their friends that used them for David's sake but if he overindulged, Susan would get furious. David tried to explain along with some of the other wives that this was acceptable now days.

Their friends delved into the Age of Aquarius, horoscopes and astrology. Susan didn't consider herself, or David to be hippies, although they had adapted to the casual dress style and Susan appreciated the bra-less attire for women. She adored the natural fabrics and home spun design of their clothing, when they weren't working professionally. David grew his hair longer and Susan let hers grow, adapting to the easier care styles. Susan didn't have any religious upbringing so she believed all this hocus pocus was nonsense. Although she appreciated much of the style through the time frame they were living, David would never convince her that mind altering drugs could make already creative people more creative. She even admitted to David she felt she was out of step with modern thinking but still didn't want to mess around with chemicals in her body.

Susan noticed after her second miscarriage that David developed a short-fuse. She tried to talk with him but he responded that work overwhelmed him. He experienced nightmares, and felt frightened by what life brought him. He told her the last vision he had before boarding the plane home from Vietnam was families being torn apart by the war. There were American G.I.'s who married foreign girls. They were told by the communists that if the women got on the plane to come to the United States with their new husbands and children, they would never see their families again. They also told them they could never return or they could be killed. Many changed their minds at the last minute and abandoned their children and American husbands. They ran down the steps of the departing planes and back into the arms of their blood relatives on the ground. David observed men crying. Some cried for their families, some for deceased friends, and some from sheer relief that the war was officially over and they made it back to the United

States and their homes. Many felt guilty that they had survived when their buddies didn't. David cried himself as he saw the soldiers and their comrades spat upon and cussed at as they stumbled off the returning planes. The poor soldiers humbled and humiliated. This war, more than any other in history was full of confusion and self-doubt.

David felt compelled to shake their hands and thank them. Most could only respond by mumbling and shaking back. They were numb. David wrote in one of his articles that the atmosphere surrounding the returning soldiers felt of heavy despair and depression. David believed that this was not at all like World War II. The boys returned home together and fought together as a team. The war now was on an individual rotation basis and lonely. David could not understand the majority of his countrymen's lack of concern, especially Susan who usually was compassionate. She just didn't understand. Most people did not understand, even the soldiers themselves. The more David struggled to get this fact out, the more he met with opposition from his peers.

"Let it go David." They advised him in their tenth year of marriage. David continued to struggle and worked up some serious concern for his fellow man, for the soldiers returning, but alone, there was nothing he could do about it.

In the spring, Susan suffered her third miscarriage, a little boy. David and Susan were distraught. They considered adopting but a year later and after much testing, it was discovered that Susan suffered from a disease called lupus. She was poked and pried so much that they made the decision to put off future plans for children. David was disappointed. He wanted a son to carry on the family name.

Susan's body burned out of hormones and because of miss-diagnosis, the disease had progressed rapidly. Aggressive treatment was needed to get her back on her feet.

David remembered a book he read in the Sixties called "*1984*", by George Orwell. A futuristic novel seemed unreal then but as time went on, he was beginning to see how truthful the book was in future predictions.

Chapter 9

    Susan had gone through two placebo study groups on the East Coast and she had her hip replaced because the prednisone dosage was so high she was losing calcium. A new test called a bone density showed clearly that the medications she took were affecting her body in a negative way.

    One evening Susan approached David. "Honey we need a change, could we talk about it? You've been a reporter for over twenty years. Is it possible you could retire and we could take some time together?"

    David set down his paper and pipe together, directing his attention to her. "Maybe you are right."

    Susan was surprised, most of the time he snapped at her if she interrupted his reading or writing time. He recently purchased a new computer and she worried about his long hours and wondered where he was in all those chat-rooms. She shivered as she tried to expel feelings of unattractiveness and inadequacy out of her mind.

    "Well, what is it Susan?"

    Susan answered, "Nothing." She knew David loved her despite her perceptions which were often over-dramatized because of her pain killers, still...she often felt alone and frightened. Every day she mentally faced this dreaded little known disease.

"Okay," David tipped back his chair and clasped his hands behind him. "I remember the last visit with your rheumatologist who discovered the climate may be adding to the problem. We could move back to the West Coast somewhere if you like. I think he said that was more comfortable for you. Maybe the Gulf Coast would help, but that still could be too humid. I know winters are harsh here. We could still do winter sports in the Sierras."

"You could still do them," Susan corrected him folding her arms. "Skiing and skating aren't at the top of my list anymore."

"I'm sorry Susan. I keep getting my hopes up when you have periods of remission. The incision on your leg is hardly noticeable any more from where the doctors replaced your hip." David touched her leg gently.

Susan smiled at his sudden perception. "Yes, medical science has come a long way and sometimes I do feel better. Thank-goodness." She sighed. "Every day I work hard to gain more of my strength back."

David and Susan talked and planned far into the night. Susan felt closer to her husband than she had in a long time.

The next three months were full of packing up twenty years of belongings. David's boss talked him into staying with the news company for one more year if he let him move out west and if he would be willing to do various assignments on a news arising basis anywhere in the world. David and Susan agreed to the offer. The moving process went smoothly and their house sold quickly. The Lake Placid home they were able to rent and his sister and brother-in-law purchased his half of the family home.

David and Susan found a little bungalow in Calistoga, California to rent until they could decide where they wanted to settle down. The Northern California town was exactly what the couple needed. They were only a couple of hours north of San Francisco and Susan could walk anywhere around town that she wished. Santa Rosa was only thirty minutes away and David could fly from there anytime he was called to do an assignment. Once or twice a month he needed to be in New York to submit work. They were happy and Susan hoped David could begin to relax. She felt relieved that he agreed to this new lifestyle. She occupied herself with painting classes, wine-cooking, and photography. David agreed to take a photography class with her after they purchased a new camera for family use. He wanted to be updated on the new equipment that was on the market as well. Susan slept better than she had in many years.

Chapter 10

David returned to New York just after the New Year. He was supposed to report in with the latest information on the Oakland Fires the previous October. Many insurance problems surfaced through the rebuilding process, and before that event there had been a big quake on the West Coast. People were upset that their claims were not settled fast enough. They were being put off and not getting the amounts of insurance money that they thought they would. Insurance companies excused their lack of effectiveness due to the number of claims.

He also met up with another group of people.

"Hey guys, come on. You know I can only do so much. It's not easy to do a juggling act all the time. You have always gotten the goods. Your chemicals and drugs are basically what you want. The software is ready to go and I can deliver and set up the equipment for each country. However, I need to do the main frame in Europe for the banking part of things. The research crews tell me that the laser system is ready to go as well. Just remember your promise to me."

David addressed a well-respected group of political representatives. He breathed deep because the addictive adrenaline rush, the danger of an undercover agent, was like gambling to a gambler. He couldn't quit, he was way over his head and he realized it as he stepped onto the tarp.

A senior politician reached for his hand, "We're glad you could make it David. Most of these men, you've met personally."

"Nice to see you all as well," David acknowledged each man with a firm grip.

One of the men suggested they walk to an air conditioned Limousine where they could finish their conversation comfortably in a short period of time.

David climbed in and said, "A trip to Europe is needed in the near future, and I'll need to have someone from this group to meet me there."

"Ah yes," the Senior Senator twiddled his thumbs together, "We should meet again in three months; I believe that gives us enough time to polish up our final plans."

"That works for the rest of us, right everyone?" A tall, purposeful man broke into the conversation. Clearly, the leader, he looked from one person to the next for agreement. "I assure you that our plan will not fail, we finally have people in Europe ready to meet with David, whomever we choose to meet with him there. The group shook hands and agreed to meet again in three months. A plan that had been in process for over a hundred years continued to move forward.

David said, "This will go fast once we begin to connect the dots, it'll be over soon." He shook his head and waved as he moved out of the vehicle and waved, headed toward the waiting airplane.

Chapter 11

Fog rolled in off the bay as Susan pulled to the pick-up curb, just in time. David's plane had arrived late, landing on slick tarmac. They decided to spend the night and have dinner on the wharf. Susan shivered as the sun went down. She said little during dinner.

David said, "What's wrong honey?" He patted her hand. "Are you cold? Perhaps we should eat inside one of the nicer restaurants?" David guided her inside to a warm inviting dining area.

"I'm tired David. That's all," she sighed. "I had a premonition. I fear for you. You are gone more than I expected when we moved here." She dropped her gaze low and played with the napkin placed in her lap. "Maybe I need to go and have my blood work checked. We've been here a year now and I've been putting off seeking a rheumatologist. I hear there is a wonderful up-to-date lady doctor in Santa Rosa. She's has a fine reputation and is successful in her practice."

She smiled and reached across the table to touch his hand. "You must be tired too David, you can share more with me. You know, with all the traveling that you do, maybe you should get a physical as well. There are some excellent doctors in our area."

"Now," David whined. "We've been through this before. I'm fine. I just have a little jet-lag. I've been doing this for so many years, a drink or two will just put a little kick back in the mule."

"Before I forget, David, I have us signed up for a photography class at the Santa Rosa Junior College," Susan advised.

"Well when is it?" David asked. "You know... I'm on a tight schedule."

"The class starts in a couple of weeks." She smiled. "We should be finishing up when the early spring foliage begins to bloom."

David toasted to a new experience for her, "A photography class will be fun for you, and I'll join when I can. We'll have a good time together." He reminded her that he still wanted to get some updated information on the latest photography and video equipment that would soon be on the market. Hand in hand, with a feeling of sincere joy, they walked back to their hotel for the rest of the evening.

Driving through Napa Valley the following day, they took their time and tasted wine on their way. They ate lunch at a delightful sidewalk café, splurging on a tasty Merlot and exotic delicacies before they picked up groceries on their way home.

"It's chilly this evening David, would you please light the fire?" Susan called from the kitchen. She came into the living room carrying a platter of fruits, breads, and cheeses. A bottle of their favorite wine, chilled to perfection, and Susan drank until she was tipsy David was amused and dismayed. He enjoyed her advances and decided he wouldn't spoil a good evening. He would talk with her in the morning, this was unlike her and he was concerned.

David woke Susan with coffee in one hand and an Alka-seltzer in the other.

"Wow," Susan exclaimed holding her head and sipping her

coffee. "As bad as I feel, I figure you would like an Alka-seltzer too."

David laughed, "Yes, as a matter of fact, but I don't need it. Coffee will be fine; it's only twice as strong as you normally brew it! By the way, what got into you last night? I mean you were a lot of fun. You never overindulge." By the look on Susan's face, he realized he hit a nerve.   She paused and then told him she was experiencing a lot of pain again and she hated taking her medication. So in place of it sometimes, the wine was helpful. She giggled and then tickling him, adding that it was especially true if it involved him.

He responded by pushing her back and demanded to know what was going on. She confessed that she was having trouble again in her hips and she started to cry. She told him she was scared that she would have to go back on some of the more aggressive drug treatments and that it would make her good hip worse. David remembered how grueling her first hip replacement was, she had been on the wrong medications before her diagnosis of Lupus, prednisone, and chemo damaged her bones and he realized how scared Susan had become. They argued about remission and he confessed that he didn't understand remission at all. Susan reminded him over and over that remission does not mean healed. He couldn't believe she wasn't going to get better. "I'm sorry Susan." He held her tight and told her he loved her.

***

Two weeks later, Susan was able to see her doctor and the prognosis was not good. Her medications and pain killers were increased and within a month, her limbs were swollen and she began stumbling and falling. David tried to keep life light around her but he felt overwhelmed. Last time she went through this crises, they were among family and friends. They were so busy; they hadn't taken time this past year to make new friends. David began commuting back and forth every couple of weeks to New York. Susan started protesting and complaining that she felt lonely. She wanted to go along with him once in awhile. David snapped, "Look Susan you know how hard flying is on you. Find something to do, plant a garden, go to church, and join the ladies golf club down the road. I have to get groceries but I'll be back soon." The screen door slammed shut. Susan felt hurt but she realized how helpless he felt so she busied herself with the laundry and dishes. He needed his white shirts ironed for the upcoming trip back to New York.

    David drove around town for a while before going to the store. For the first time in years, he began to sob. The car brakes squealed as he pulled over and stopped the engine, wiping the tears from his eyes. He melted; it seemed to him he was losing more power and control than ever. He knew his wife was suffering. He couldn't make Susan well and he was being pressured to make arrangements to go to Europe. For the first time since he was a child, he thought seriously about God. Once again, he entertained thoughts of abandonment. "God if you are out there, I challenge you to show yourself." He shouted to the empty space in his car and started the engine.

    David pulled up in the parking lot of the grocery store to see a beautiful golden retriever obediently tagging alongside its trainer. David jumped out and introduced himself to the dog and its companion. A gracious human smiled. She took off her straw hat and dusting her hand on her skirt, reached to shake hands with him. "Hi, I am Grace Brown and this is Lucky." She re-adjusted her leash and collar as the retriever grinned and wagged her golden tail. Since Lucky just birthed puppies Grace explained to David she was bringing her outside for a walk. David was impressed with this beautiful dog and her manners. The two people visited for awhile and David shared that they were new in town and his wife suffered from lupus and didn't get out much.

    "Well, David why don't you bring Susan by, I bet she

would love to meet Lucky and her babies. My husband would enjoy meeting you two as well."

David smiled, "The weather is so nice and I know that Susan feels cooped up. Would this evening be too early? I can see by the address you wrote down that you live a couple of blocks from us." He was pleased with her positive response.

***

As he turned into the driveway, David shouted for Susan to come out and help him with the lighter items. He grabbed her and picked her up. "Honey, I'm sorry honest. I know I was short. Forgive me? I have a surprise for you after dinner. I want you to meet someone."

Susan hugged him. "It's okay David. I know life is frustrating. Where are you taking me? What should I wear?"

"Your levis are perfect." David kissed her soundly on the lips as he answered.

"Yum, this chicken salad was perfect for dinner; you are a good shopper David." Susan grinned. "I am so excited, I can hardly finish eating." She wiped her mouth with her napkin. "I'm finished. I'll clean the kitchen before we go."

"Let's walk Susan. You can hold onto me if you need to. The house is nearby," David suggested to her.

"What a wonderful idea David, I'll just get my sweater." Susan hurried to the front room closet.

The evening was full of pleasant sounds and the air was fragrant with a half-moon rising in the early twilight. The sun still hadn't set so the sky was full of golden hues and rainbow jet trails. A piece of violet cloud brushed the horizon.

Grace and Lucky greeted them as they came up the steps. Susan exclaimed, "What a beautiful dog, may I pet her?"

Grace responded cheerfully that Lucky loved to be petted. She invited them inside to meet the rest of her family and Mr.

Brown. "Chris," she called to her husband. "David and Susan have arrived." Chris came from the living room and he pumped first David's hand and then Susan's.

"Where is the rest of your family?" Susan asked.

Grace grinned and put her arm around Susan guiding her to the laundry room where a box with three puppies filled a corner. They were six weeks old and just waking from their naps. At the sound of Susan's voice they jumped up. Lucky gently stepped into the box and placed herself between her babies and the new people. "Oh Lucky, what a good mom you are." Susan gave her a pet on the forehead. "May I hold one?"

"Yes," Grace answered. "But give her a few minutes. She knows what you want. As soon as she feels comfortable with you, she'll leave them and go into the living room with Chris and David."

They all chatted about current events, puppies and sunsets. The sipped their coffee and ate the most delicious apple nut cake. Lucky flopped across Chris's feet. Grace told them to watch her as she brought the three babies out and they all took turns playing with them. Soon they were yawning and ready for more milk and naps. Lucky dutifully trotted off with Grace to put them to bed.

The new friends visited for a while longer. Grace was a hostess at one of the local vineyards and Chris was a buyer in Santa Rosa for a computer company. They volunteered to raise puppies and train working dogs for a national organization. Susan and David knew of guide dogs for the blind. Chris laughed as he explained there are many different breeds of dogs that help many different types of medical problems. Not only are they companions for their people but help them physically as well.

"There are many volunteers too that do a variety of things," Grace added. "Perhaps Susan would like to go with me to one of the graduating classes. There is one in Santa Rosa next week." After learning what a graduating class was all about, Susan agreed, eager to attend the next one.

David sighed, happy that he made such a good decision in meeting Chris and Grace. He would let Susan go at her own speed as far as getting involved, but he sensed this was a good thing for her. Maybe he could get her one of these companions. Grace explained there was a long waiting list but some dogs wash out of the program, which was very stringent and they needed good homes too. He never felt such a soft coat on a dog. Chris and Grace kept their dogs immaculate. *Maybe Susan might like to be a puppy raiser which required her to take one and prepare it for its' human? Maybe, he mused, a job like Grace, where the breeder dog came for a period of time to get pregnant and have her babies with her until they are weaned. That might help Susan's maternal needs. She needed to focus on something that needed her.*

***

The phone blinked, full of messages when David and Susan returned home. He began thinking about the following week.

Chapter 12

Two weeks later, David drove home from San Francisco in their shiny, black Mercedes. Susan ran outside to greet him. "Hi, I didn't expect you until tomorrow."

He wearily exited from the car. "The boss let me leave early because one of his kids needed to go to Washington D.C. for some school Presidential thing," David replied. He figured he would get some rest and think how he would break the news to Susan that he had to go to Europe for at least a month. A shower and Martini later, David fell into bed.

Susan cleaned up, worried that this schedule didn't seem much like retirement planning at all. David seemed to be increasing his hours rather than decreasing. They hadn't even been given time to look around for other interesting job possibilities. David could retire full time now. Susan wondered why he was hanging on to things so tightly. However, she understood his love for the news world.

***

"Wake up, Susan. Good morning," David was standing over her with coffee. The sun danced in patterns around the room, shining through the trees outside their window. David expected a great day. "I thought we could take off and go to Reno, Nevada for a couple of days." He plopped down next to her on their bed. "I need to go to Beale Air Force Base and drop off a couple of things my Dad left for an old Air Force buddy. My sister found him and contacted him." David hoped Susan would buy into his story, which thankfully, she did. She was distracted by the idea taking of a trip somewhere.

"We can take the cameras and get some good shots." She agreed so he kissed her and suggested they pack enough for a couple of days. He reminded her to include some warm clothing.

Soon after breakfast they were on the road. Susan told him what a wonderful dog graduation ceremony she had seen. She explained it was emotional and full of love on both the human and dog sides. It was a time when each dog reached certain levels in life and could go on to the next training level or be matched to their new needy owners. It was also a time of retirement for some animals and then there were options to go back to the original handlers. Susan had decided to learn the training process and take care of the breeder dogs. She wasn't sure if she would be accepted or not because of her own physical needs but she wanted to try. David listened and told her he would support her decisions and sign whatever agreements were needed.

He made small talk about his work and Susan never questioned his stories. He asked about the photography class. She told him she was enjoying them and learning quite a bit.

"Susan," David began. "I have to go Europe for awhile. It's a big story, all about the growth of computers and world-wide networking." He hoped if he used computer terminology that maybe she wouldn't be too curious. "I've been telling you all along if I can get some things in place, then I can kick back. And then Susan, I can literally run things from the house. Perhaps within five years this will all be completed. I know it's been rough, but the payoff is far bigger than you could ever imagine. Just awhile longer and then I won't have to leave you again baby," David pleaded.

Susan's eyes filled with tears as she tried to respond, "David, we have talked about this for the past two years and you keep pushing the time out. I don't understand. What happened to the dream of working independently?"

David thought hard, "Gosh Susan the news is run differently now. Local newspapers are fed from the conglomerate news world. The only things that are local are births, deaths, police logs, and spousal problems. It's pretty dull huh? I would be bored out of my mind Suzy," David complained. Susan agreed with him, it made a lot of sense to him anyway.

***

David passed through the Air Force Gate easily on his VIP pass and was told Colonel Sawyer was expecting him at Base Operations out on the runway. David breathed a sigh of relief; he never expected this to be so simple. Susan remembered that this was a Strategic Air Command Base because her father was in the Air Force. It was not an easy base to get onto. David was also relieved when Susan agreed to stay in the car. He took the camera and case so he could get a picture of the old Blackbird plane in an adjoining hanger. Once inside with Colonel Sawyer, they shot an entire roll of equipment that an average person would never see. He slipped the spent roll in his pocket and replaced it; shooting a couple of unimportant shots and making sure Colonel Sawyer and he were not in them. He gave the Colonel some paperwork and received some in return. Shaking hands, they completed their assignments. Colonel Sawyer explained to David how to get off base the back way and continue to Reno.

They stopped off half-way for a late lunch at a back road diner. Susan shivered from the spring air of a high altitude. "Want me to pull a sweater for you honey?" David asked. The valley was hot and David could see Susan was swelling. She hadn't complained and David didn't realize how uncomfortable she had become. He loved the heat and the sunshine always felt good to him. He regretted not thinking to turn on the air conditioner in their vehicle. He didn't feel cold either so he realized the Lupus was probably flaring. He would keep an eye on her and try to encourage her to rest. She napped the last hour before they got to Reno.

David pulled into the drive of their hotel before dinner. He suggested that they rest and maybe go for a swim in the indoor pool which refreshed Susan immediately. David enjoyed the sauna and hot tub. They called for room service for a quiet relaxing evening. David promised they would do dinner and dancing the following night.

Sightseeing in Virginia City, Nevada, they picked up some family Christmas presents and shot up more film.

They enjoyed their time together, but Susan was done with dancing an hour after dinner so they returned to their room. David tucked her into bed and then slipped down to the casino for a few hands of blackjack which he soon lost. He wandered around awhile and realized the colorful sights and scenes that once attracted him seemed old and seedy.

David left Susan the following week for three days of final planning for the European trip. He promised when he returned; they would go to the coast to do more photography.

Chapter 13

David arrived in his New York hotel room around midnight from the airport. Exhausted, he loosened his tie and flopped onto the king sized bed. The next morning a taxi took him from the airport hotel to the main office of a familiar news station and then straight to an undisclosed government office for an itinerary of upcoming events. David could plug his final work in France the following week. A huge computer system such as this would serve the world and take its citizens to the final cash-less society. He was on the cutting edge of implementing the beginning of the end of the New World Order. He was ecstatic about the part he played, and felt important by his collaboration with such high powered political leaders. Excited, he thought of future possibilities. He thought, they were unlimited, yet he was also afraid of new unexplored territories. If things got in the wrong hands, there would surely be harm to millions of innocent people. Suddenly, he felt worried about what he'd designed. He shrugged it off determined not to be concerned over such trivial matters.

David crawled under the covers, but since he couldn't fall asleep, he channel surfed through the motel selection on television. No matter what number he hit there was something about God on every channel. He flipped to a channel where he believed the news was coming on. Stretching and yawning he turned down the volume and drifted into an uneasy sleep.

He jerked awake a short while later to a chorus of beautiful music. Bleary eyed, David opened his eyes wider to a station that signed off the air earlier. He rolled out of bed and slipped into a robe. He poured a fresh hot cup of coffee, which he did not make, and stared intently at a Christian speaker that appeared on the television screen. He couldn't believe his ears. The man seemed to be speaking directly to him. He called David by name and pleaded with him to listen. David rubbed his eyes again and tried to change channels but the changer seemed broken. Surprised, he heard the speaker ask him to read the Bible, to read carefully and to accept Jesus Christ as his personal savior. The speaker challenged David to re-consider the negative ramifications of a one-world government.

***

The phone on the nightstand rang loudly and the hotel operator begged David to wake up. This was, she explained, his third wake-up call in the past thirty minutes. "Sir, you have asked me to call you back every five minutes. Are you okay? Your flight is leaving in half an hour. Would you like me to call a taxi?" David assured her he was awake and that her offer would be wonderful. He got into the shower but couldn't get beyond slow motion. He yawned several times and attempted some sit-ups and toe touches, as he tried to wake up and shake off his confusion. Before he knew it, the taxi had arrived to take him to the airport to his next destination. David fell asleep as soon as he sat in his assigned seat with the previous nights telecast still whirling in his mind.

David and one photographer were whisked away in a protected limo to the White House where they met with the Commander-In-Chief of the United States. The meeting was brief and formal. David, the photographer and a White House correspondent would put together the breaking news to go with a ribbon-cutting ceremony two days after implementation. The ceremony would take place together with each country's leaders to form a new world alliance. This would supersede all other pacts including the United Nations. Once the announcement was made to the World, then physical identifications would begin. The plan was to be completed and everything documented within three months. Most countries were compliant and had been moving forward for the last several years. The United States was a forerunner in the use of social security numbers. They were successful in gun control along with a strong dictator "elite" type military that was committed to this cause.

    The biggest problem David's alliances were dealt was convincing people to accept a mark on their bodies that they could utilize into the system. Leaders had come up with many ideas to get people onboard with the computer use and mass internet monitoring that would bring them incentive to join the order. Many brought the unsuspecting public face to face with their destination of using home computers for no-fee checking, paying their bills automatically through direct deposit, no interest on home and vehicle loans plus many better deals on charge cards. Soon people needed to have home computers to be able to do business and daily living transactions. The public believed it was safer to go to the computer-bank in the safety of their homes. Banking transactions versus teller machines at night, outside on the street corner made a lot more sense.

    David's associates came up with ideas to bring people to accept using an identification mark. The first step he took was to horrify parents with good job stamps on the back of public school children's hands. Of course, the ink would wash off. Stamping, then stenciling was a fad among children and their peers during the seventies and eighties. Many teen idols sported tattoos and they became more acceptable and common in the eighties, and nineties. It became vogue to have an indiscreet little fairy on ones' ankle or shoulder. Little by little, American Society allowed tattoos to become common place, accepting what some considered the inevitable mark of the beast without even realizing.

David figured people; especially vain women would be more willing to be marked if they had choices. He suggested telling them the bar-code could be on their foreheads or hands, or could be visible, better yet, invisible? People might like a choice of sparkling beautiful colors that would show up under laser light? That idea could become the fashion statement of the new millennium.

Brilliant David, moved quickly into leadership of his association which he believed was serving his country. He was proud to serve. Rumors around Washington D.C. indicated that he was the Presidents' right-hand man. He could always come up with reasons that made sense to move the public forward.

There were a few people in the F.B.I. regular system that were die-hards and didn't want to go that direction. They believed the United States was Sovereign and should stay independent. The President was concerned, but David felt confident that those individuals were few and could be convinced over time. Too many people with conflicting ideas worked in the government.

***

The country's Vice-President was horrified; he hadn't realized things had gone as far ahead as they had. He didn't believe they, as a country, should be moving ahead so fast. He saw firsthand the power displayed in a laser ring that was presented to his boss on his fiftieth birthday. He resolved to get out of office as soon as possible. Circles in Washington D.C. were saying he was crazy, why he even started to go to prayer meetings! Any religious activity beyond Sundays was considered fanatical.

Chapter 14

David called, "Hey Susan, how are you? Can you pick me up in Santa Rosa this evening around dinner time?" He shook his head, "No, I'm feeling rough and want to go straight home. Maybe it's the flu. Every time I stand up, I feel dis-orientated and am experiencing some vertigo." He didn't want to share that he'd been blacking out for several minutes at a time and couldn't remember the drive home. With Susan's help, he fell into bed and within seconds was asleep.

Susan was aware that he suffered some problems, but every time she mentioned the subject, he became angry, almost violent. She didn't realize how bad his health had become. His secret had remained hidden. She figured maybe he was getting a little older and the jet lag lasted longer. The result of three straight martinis from Salt Lake City, Utah never occurred to David or Susan. She hadn't known.

***

As promised, David went with Susan as often as possible to her photography class. So, the following Wednesday, they attended. The class proved interesting to David. This one concentrated on laser lights and the things one could do with film.

Saturday, the couple planned a trip to the coast. They would take lots of film and spend the night. "Oh David, the spring flowers are so pretty." Susan clapped her hands together. They enjoyed brunch at the wharf and David drank more than usual at dinner, and continued to drink afterward.

"Please don't drink too much today, David," Susan pleaded. "I'm uncomfortable with these narrow curvy roads."

"Susan, don't worry so much. I'm fine." David scowled. She knew then, that she had pushed too far and remained quiet. They headed north up Highway 1 to Goat Rock Beach where they'd seen multicolored ice-plant all over the hills and along the parking lot.

"David put that thing out," Susan requested. "The smell is terrible. That can't possibly be a regular cigarette." She wrinkled her nose and waved her hand in the air.

David lit up again as soon as he opened the car door and stumbled as he came around to open Susan's door. "Susan, I'm still drowsy from the trip, this will help me wake up. The air is fresh and breezy, this is great." And he straightened his posture and inhaled deeply as if to show her how much better he was beginning to feel. "Now don't be so darned difficult."

Susan asked, "What's wrong?" but then taken aback by his quick personality change but she remained quiet. She noticed he had a strange look across his face. It was contorted and his eyes were mean and glaring. She shivered in fright at his face. The last thing Susan remembered was David's glowing yellow snake eyes as he dropped her into the icy waters below.

***

David looked down into the crashing waves not wanting, but almost hoping to see Susan's body. He was thankful that his tears were sincere. He believed he'd done the right thing for both of them. She was becoming too demanding of his time and he really didn't have many more excuses. His wife would never consider moving to Washington D.C. or overseas. Although he loved her, he didn't think she would live this long. He was in too deep and he needed to keep moving forward or they may have both died.

David waited until almost noon before he dialed 911 on his cell phone. He blacked out as soon as he returned to the car. He remembered very little of what happened. Susan must have slipped in the dew filled ice-plants, she fell and David couldn't catch her.

Search and rescue came immediately, but thick fog rolled inland and weather conditions changed drastically. A late spring storm swept the coast and by five in the evening, the search was called off. David returned to Bodega Bay where he kept his overnight reservations, but there was no change in the weather for the next three days. Susan was presumed dead, lost at sea.

He was exhausted and confused. His brain was in overdrive and arguments to justify his actions burned in his mind for the next week. Nightmares strung him out more and more. He turned to the smokes, the liquor, and tried to convince himself that he couldn't hold her. He tried to convince himself, as he had the police that he'd dropped her accidently, that she'd slid from his hands.

Once David was home, he called Susan's sister, her parents, his boss, only a few people with a need to know and discouraged them from coming. He would have a quiet memorial at the site and asked that Susan's wishes be honored. Everything was to go to the Lupus Foundation to help with research. Busy fast- paced lives were the only type people David and Susan knew so his request was gratefully acknowledged.

Loose ends were tied up and David was on his way to Europe with no break in his original schedule.

Chapter 15

David boarded Air Force One out at Moffett Air Field that night. He barely had enough time to clean up and pack a fresh set of clothing. He traveled with the President as one of the reporters under the guise of a political rally. A story written months earlier explained the reason; to search out individuals who might be future problems. Most of the work included data entry and few very low key interviews. Christian Coalition was sharing some unsettling news to those followers concerned about the fast paced changes; they needed assurance that all was well on the home front. Those with a vested interest calmed concerns by attempting to cause fear among the public that this group could be a possible cult. Hawaii and the west coast were always the best places to start rumors of this type.

David was handed an itinerary as he boarded. The First Family was going together this trip. They planned to drop their son at the University of Hawaii. There would be the rally and then a couple of down days for the Chief Executive and his wife. The First Lady hated to fly over the ocean during the day and so they accommodated her and flew during the night time.

"You know David, we are so sorry to hear about your wife." The President shook his hand as he boarded the plane, and he pulled him into a bear hug.

"Thanks," David replied. "It has been rough, I loved her so much. Maybe it's for the best." He paused and then added, "At least she's not going to have to suffer any longer."

There. He'd said it. Now he felt more convinced.

A sharp clean-cut, man with dark wavy hair, Vice-President Jim Lewis, encouraged him. "Ah yes, the Lupus, you mentioned she was having trouble stumbling from the weakness of her other hip and leg muscles. Well, now you know you are with family. You come to Washington and spend a couple of days with us and the kids."

David replied that he would consider the invitation and thanked him. With the exception of the Browns, the Vice-President and his family seemed the only sincere people in his life. He and Susan knew many social acquaintances, but had few friends. Either they were too busy or shallow to spend time with them. Susan's counselor mentioned to her that people became afraid to be around life-threatening diseases. They would look at the person as a mirror of themselves and many were unable to handle their feelings of inadequacy and fear.

***

David was relieved to take off in the air at last. He played a couple of hands of bridge and after excusing himself with a drink in his hand, he returned to his seat and extended it as far as it would go for some needed sleep. .

He woke with a start as the plane hit the runway and taxied to the concourse. He re-positioned himself and fell back to sleep. The sun was already up when he woke the second time. He stretched and yawned, mumbling to himself, "Feels good, I can't remember the last time I got eight hours of sleep. Phooey! I forgot my tie for this evening. Now I've got to go buy one."

The following week was spent in Europe, implementing the system and flipping switches. An entire day was devoted to a ceremony and uniting of the ten countries involved. A changeover of power completed with much pomp and circumstance, world leaders religious leaders and the Pope attended. Of course, there were the usual dissenters and rallies. Many small organized groups protested, but they were shut down quickly by pre-planned militia. The leaders stated their relief that none of the groups were very large or able to get their point across to the unsuspecting world.

The last meeting the New World Order had was to plan and begin the next step. All their satellites were in place. They needed to put into use, the new system with televisions, computers, and telephones so "Big Brother" could monitor everyone. The idea was suggested in the early part of the twentieth century and little by little, people fell into place, like sheep being led to slaughter. David once again used materialism and ego to convince people they needed his new technology to keep up in this fast-paced world. They didn't need weapons when the government offered a wonderful safe way of centralizing a home security system. The Sheriff could be at your home in seconds to protect you! Then you would never have to worry about your children getting guns and harming each other.

Socialized medicine for all became the next strategy. The baby-boomers signed up for health care, the next generation followed. David believed the medical phase could be finalized by 2010 depending on the people who argued and worked to undo damage. The whole system of government and what it meant had to be re-structured. People fought hard to have their choices apart from the government. The only alternative the government had was to break up the HMOS and with the FDA's help, charge so much for drugs that people and doctors would be crying for help. Big Brother of course, came up with solutions and right answers. Medicine could be purchased at reduced prices and doctor bills could be paid through billing medical companies, health services, and pharmacies on the computer.

If one didn't have a computer or at least know how to use one, they would soon be lost. They would have no way to function in society for even the basic necessities of life.

Big Brother was after was the public school system. The whole business went broke due to deep pocket, miss-managed funds, and illiterate children. The only real training the younger generation received was about how to use computers and how to exercise your right to do your own thing. The word responsibility meant nothing. The poor latch-key children had nothing to do after school, except to sit home by themselves or find trouble, if they didn't go home. They were unmotivated to do anything if they weren't gifted in understanding computers or sports. All the music, art, and literature programs no longer existed in public schools. Some home schooled children were fortunate enough to be able to play an instrument and some of the remaining private schools offered individual lessons after school hours. A concerned parent was quickly assured that as long as a child knew how to use the internet or as it was called, the information highway, they could find anything they liked to learn about. Therefore, they obtained a far superior education to their parents. In fact, teachers told students how ignorant their parents were and breed a new type of disrespect for elders bringing new definition to generation gap. They should have learned from past history what happens when the old are despised. The only problem was that most of the history was missing from informative reading material. Many baby boomers were poor readers as well. Proper vocabulary and grammar skills fell to simple phrases and spelling with as few letters as possible. Most parents and adults had trouble keeping up with the poor "newer" language of the younger generation.

One problem that went unnoticed was the realization that children were taught as miniature soldiers, lacking individual recognition and training. Everyone screamed for more money for better programs, more pay, updated materials, and better, bigger buildings. Children went to school in trailers on site. The insulation, sound, electricity, and lighting were poor.

Insurance rates climbed out of control, gas prices skyrocketed, and the weather became increasingly unpredictable. Fear prevailed around the world. Anyone saying the wrong thing at the wrong time could be legally liable. Cash incentives were offered to those who would report suspicious behaviors and actions of their neighbors. Big Brother was always there to "make things better." Everything had to be politically correct.

David constantly wrote and re-wrote articles that soothed the people. He and five other heads of networks wrote together and wired the latest news out to their assigned papers and news stations. Everyone around the world received the same information.

During the constant unfolding chaos, a new world-wide disease revealed itself in medical centers everywhere. This disease was much worse than AIDS. People avoided socializing as in past generations, which caused their immune systems to be compromised. Until now, the population hadn't been exposed to many germs and viruses; therefore they were more susceptible than ever to new strains that came along. Polio, measles, and a type of smallpox returned, with a vengeance. Those diseases, at least most of them were eradicated from the United States. Young doctors had never seen these diseases or their symptoms. Tuberculosis re-appeared. Germ warfare came up often in conversation. David wondered about Lupus and some of the other new diseases. Did they just show up or had they always been around under different names? So many people suffered the same symptoms which made it very difficult for the doctors to diagnose and treat with the proper medications.

Chapter 16

David took a week off after his trip to Europe. He notified the President, and his editor in New York City of his intentions to check in with them for any daily calls. He requested that they not call unless an emergency came up. His superiors agreed. The trip proved to be long and hard but it was successful and everyone slowed down for awhile.

***

David drank and slept for two straight days after he returned home to Calistoga. He lost track of time. Waking up from alcohol and jet lag, he checked the messages on his telephone and decided to go out for some groceries. He walked and drank in grape scented air as it swirled in a light breeze. Color filled the space around him. Trees rich endowed with autumns chill, graced every layer of the rolling valley, ripe for stomping, the sweet aromatic grape scent wafted across his path. He thought it might be fun to drop in at the fairgrounds and check out the fall fair. People celebrated in every part of the community. The valley slowed for autumn. School started and there were retired people in motor homes parked along the streets.

A balmy evening filled the valley on the eve David returned home. A bright sun settled into the western sky as the orange harvest moon rose. The sky took on the colors of a rainbow, splintering and weaving, the aurora borealis danced overhead as the leaves chattered in the breezes through old oak and pine trees.

Mr. and Mrs. Brown left a message for David to return their call when he returned.

"Hi Chris, how are you?" David switched the phone to his other ear to hear better.

"We're just fine David, how about you? The wife and I saw your car in the driveway and realized you were home. We would love to have you for dinner tomorrow night if you're available?"

David graciously accepted, "Thanks guys I could use some nice company. Can I bring anything, perhaps a bottle of wine?"

"Grace says she has everything. Thanks. See you about six or so," Chris hung up the phone.

David arrived as sprinkles of rain fell on his nose. The walk felt good in the damp foggy air.

"First rain of the season coming in," Chris spoke as he shook David's hand. Lucky wagged her tail to welcome him.

David nodded in agreement.

Grace ran from the kitchen and hugged David tightly. "We are so glad to see you," She said as she untied her apron. "Here you two, have some wine and cheese while Chris stirs the fire in the living room.

"Something sure smells wonderful," David held his nose high in the air and laughed.

"Oh my," Grace set the cheese on the table and turned around, "I didn't remember to set the timer. Everything is ready. I'll pull the roast, it'll need to sit for a few minutes before Chris can carve it and David will you light the dinner candles for me? You boys go ahead and seat yourselves; it should be about fifteen minutes before I'm ready with the rest of the dinner. Thanks!" She shouted on the way to the kitchen.

Lucky got up from the fire, yawned and stretched. Trotting after Chris, she sat next to his chair. "Now Lucky, you know the rules; no people food. If you are nice and don't beg you can stay in the dining room and I'll bring your food in here." Chris spoke firmly; Lucky obeyed and let out a long sigh while she slid to the floor.

Chris and Grace grabbed David's hands on either side of him to pray as they sat down. For the first time, David felt comfortable enough to let his guard down. He felt like he could confide in these people. Dinner conversation revolved around Lucky. The last litter had just been weaned and taken to the next phase of their training. She had been moping around for a couple of days but coming out of it, Grace explained to David. There was an upcoming graduation for one of her older puppies.

Susan was hardly mentioned. The couple told him how very sorry they hadn't been more help to him, but he left so fast, they felt at a loss as to what he needed.

"David, you're quiet," Grace commented. "Is everything okay? It seems to us that you're exhausted, perhaps we can help in some way?"

David replied, "Thanks, I am tired. I've been burning the candle at both ends for far too long. The food is wonderful tonight and I'm enjoying your company." He made an effort to eat a little more although he felt a lump in his throat and no appetite.

Chris pushed back his chair and folded his napkin and pushed it into the brass holder. Then he offered a glass of brandy by the living room fire.

David sank into an overstuffed chair and sighed, putting his head down between his hands. Alarmed, Grace spoke, "David what is it? What's wrong?"

"I don't understand. Everything seems so out of control. I miss Susan so much and I guess I've been so busy there has been no time for the grief process," his eyes brimmed with tears that rolled slowly down his cheeks.

Chris responded with, "Talk to us David and let it go. You know we are here for you. Susan was a special lady to all of us."

The warm company and a golden retriever kissing his hand was all it took for David to begin pouring his heart out. He knew he was on dangerous ground. He was sharing high level secrets, but he trusted these people and he needed to talk with someone. He explained how he had been involved in the development of a New World Government for the past twenty years or so. He told of working for two masters, living a double life and manipulating much of the world news. He shared about his drug usage. The night the television evangelist spoke to him and he began to believe he had been slipped something in either the drugs or alcohol he had consumed because he started blacking out. "I'm scared," David confided. "I don't have any re-call of events that happened to me. Susan's body was flaring up again. She was hurting so badly and facing surgery on the other hip. I was coming off a bad trip when we went to the coast and I...I dropped her, I couldn't save her. I thought I was doing her a favor." David sobbed hysterically as he began to confess and pour out his feelings of guilt.

"Oh David, we are so sorry." Chris spoke as he put his arms around him. David realized how much they understood. He questioned them as to how and why they could understand what he was saying. They talked through the night.

"Nothing you've told us about the New World Order is a surprise to us David," the couple admitted to him. "The Bible is full of insight as to the way the world operates, past, present and future. We are not experts, just believers in Jesus Christ. True believers are interested in what Jesus has to say in the Bible. He is the same forever," Grace spoke.

"Thank goodness for some consistency in this old world. You sound as if this person is alive," David raised one eyebrow and wrung his hands together.

"Well yes... He is. Those stories are true my friend. He is alive. He lives in our hearts because we invited Him to live there. He directs our lives for the good of ourselves and fellow man, if we listen to Him and follow His advice. It's our choice though as to whether we want a personal relationship or not," Chris answered.

"If what you say is true, then I want that too. I want what you've got," David requested.

"It is so simple, David, like opening a Christmas present. You have to take an active part in this relationship. You are the one who has to sincerely invite Jesus into your heart and ask Him to forgive you for your sin and desire a personal relationship with Him. I guarantee He will respond to you. You know, David, He has been calling you for a long time," Chris lovingly advised David. At David's request, Chris and Grace began to pray out loud with him. David learned that all people have sinned and need to confess to Jesus and then he gave his heart to Him.

***

David let out a long sob as the past flashed before his eyes. Yes, he remembered all those intimate times with God, even as a child. He could remember that soft, reassuring, loving presence during long hours in the hospital with Susan.

David experienced a difficult time accepting the fact that he was indeed loved and forgiven. The patient listening and sharing of his friends relieved his fears about giving his life to a higher power. He had the most trouble with forgiving himself, his past decisions, and his responsibility for Susan's death. Chris convinced him that if Jesus, being bigger, could forgive him, then he could surely forgive himself. David became free as he prayed in earnest.

Excited, David saw his life from a different perspective. "What am I going to do now?" He spoke out loud.

His friends laughed and hugged him. They advised him to listen to his heart and to stop using drugs and alcohol. Those vices could cloud issues that he would be facing in the future. The couple encouraged him to read the Bible. David asked Jesus to take away the dependency of these dangerous hooks in his life and felt immediate release.

David turned pale again. "The Vice-President, now everything is making sense. He must be a Christian."

"Perhaps David, God needs you to help and support him," Grace suggested. "I'll make some coffee."

The first rays of sunshine broke through the morning mist.

David walked home feeling clean and alive. He could smell all the wonders of fresh mountain air as he gulped deep breaths of oxygen. He read and slept for three days before he got any direction as to what he should do. He called into work and asked for another week of vacation and then called the Vice-President of the United States.

***

"Hello Sir, this is David. Can I take you up on your invitation to your home and family for Thanksgiving?"

"Why of course," answered the Second-in-Command. "Are you doing okay? The office said you were down with the flu?"

"Oh yes, I'm much better... just got overtired and I've needed to catch up on personal things in California. Thank you and Sir, please, I prefer to keep this meeting confidential," David requested carefully.

"You got it. I'll have our driver pick you up at the Denver airport on the twenty-third. Our cabin is only a couple of hours away. There's snow so pack some warm things. Bring your skis as well. I haven't been down the mountain in ages. We're looking forward to seeing you. Carol and the kids send their love David, goodbye." The Vice- President hung up.

David felt warm and welcome. This family was genuine.

Chapter 17

An hour past ETA in Denver due to blizzard conditions over the Sierra Nevada Mountains, David's flight finally landed from San Francisco.

"Hi Bob. How are you?" David extended his hand toward the driver as he stood up to open the limo door. Bob shot a funny look and grinned, this wasn't proto-call but then it was the holidays. Everyone became a little friendlier.

David dozed as the warm vehicle purred, driving into big white flakes of snow. Big white flakes swirled in the traffic, diving for the front lights and the windshield as the vehicle moved along the highway toward the mountains. Wet flakes interrupted the windshield wipers as they swiped rhythmically across the glass revealing a darkening sky. Twinkling lights filled surrounding trees, brightened the white snow and greeted David as Bob pulled into a circular driveway in front of a modest chalet. The family waited at the top of a broad woven brick porch. They hollered greetings as he made his way up the path and into the bold entry. Carol directed everyone inside while the Vice-President instructed Bob to park the vehicle in a detached garage. The home was brightly lit, with a deliciously inviting meal arranged on the dining room table. Each took their places and he was invited to sit on one side between family members. Thanksgiving Day was always a family day with minimum security, then they catered a big Christmas party during the week between Christmas and New Year's. Carol and their three daughters liked to do all the cooking. Their only son was at his grandparents near his college getting ready for exams. David felt welcome and comfortable in their home. He enjoyed the flutter and tender care he was given. He hadn't received much nurturing attention since before Susan died. The girls were well mannered and loving as they played hostess to their new guest. They hadn't seen him in a long time and being teens, they giggled and laughed. David was after all, a pretty cute guy even if he was thirty years older than them.

David observed the first day. He wasn't sure how far he could trust the Vice-President. He noticed the family prayed together at meals and there were a couple of Bibles lying around the house that appeared to be well read. The test would be when he could be alone with this friend and ask him directly.

The Vice-President did the same thing with David. He and Carol had been interceding for him for years. They realized after a long political career that things were moving fast towards a computer driven world. Jim was in a secret fraternity in college and at first; things seemed to be a big game of power and monopoly. As they raised their children, they began to see life in a different way than most of their counter-parts. Carol became stronger in her beliefs and firmly put her foot down in some of their decisions as a family. She became frightened for her husband and children. At one point, Carol even suggested a separation or worse, possible divorce. The Vice-President, then elect, decided maybe he should seriously consider this Jesus person. Things in his life seemed to be falling apart. Having reached that point, he realized changes needed to happen. Family first, then his pursuit of the job, his priorities had to change.

The President wasn't always pleased with his Vice-President, but like everything else, the guise of Christianity was used in getting the people to go along with new ideas. The Presidents' philosophy was to use the language of Christianity; a person didn't have to necessarily live that way. After all, didn't Jesus bring freedom to do as you choose, and didn't He bring protection within your Federal and State laws? As long as you obey the laws of government you'll be safe. Trust the government first because it was in place for the good of the people.

Jim and Carol were praying and desperate to leave the political world behind. The family owned a Colorado home and Jim could teach in any number of institutions.

Thanksgiving dawned bright and sunny. "Come on David; let's go out on the slopes while the girls cook." His daughters wanted to go as well, so their father assured them they could go on Saturday if they helped their mother today.

David was quite out of breath as they did a couple of slow runs down the new powdered ski-slope. He was not used to the high altitude.

"Okay, David, what's bothering you?" The Vice-President said as he handed David a bottle of water. A reserved man, David was startled at his directness. They had just gotten off the ski lift and were standing at the top of the mountain where a stiff breeze began to swirl, sending biting snow crystals into their faces. David looked down at the secret-service men following them.

He took a deep breath, and stared into Jim's eyes, equally direct as he asked, "Are you a committed Christian or not? I need to have your complete confidence before we can talk. Send those boys far away for awhile." He motioned his head towards the two approaching agents.

"Okay, David, you call the shots and I'll listen. I am committed to Jesus and so is Carol." The Vice-President met the bodyguards as they got off the lift and asked them to give David and him some space. They would be stopping several times on their way down.

David began sharing what happened to him and how he changed and now his concern was for the future of the United States. He felt he needed direction and had been praying for help. He wanted out of his situation but didn't know how or what to do.

***

Jim reminded David that as one of the President's right hand men he was being groomed for future political positions. Jim also shared that he was happy to see the change in David. Jim mentioned that David appeared to be more relaxed and the chemical dependency seemed to be gone. David was commended for taking Jim and Carol into his confidence and wanting help.

David said, "I can see how you and Carol are suffering in a lot of ways."

Jim nodded.

The two men agreed they would meet again soon and try to formulate a plan that could possibly halt the "New One World Movement."

***

"The problem is, David… the secret society is big, bigger than you can imagine. It's been around for hundreds of years. The people involved are influential and money is no object. The amounts of cash needed are there. You know what society I'm talking about. The rings we wear are significant. You're on the verge of being brought into the group and receiving your own ring. You are unusual and needed. Most men are invited to join in college. There are only about one thousand of us world-wide. I don't agree with a lot of things about them now and I only wear the ring when I have to. My college days were a joke. I didn't realize just how scary and committed the group was and is. College came easy for me and everything was play to me. Carol and I are also praying to get out of the society." Jim stopped and frowned as if thinking before he spoke again.

"We have friends and people to help us. We'll help you as well, but it is dangerous. Things will demand the right timing and lots of prayer." He paused, anxious to continue but needing David to grasp the seriousness of this information. Taking a deep breath he suggested they ski downhill a little more.

"Now is the time for you to change some of your thinking. For one thing, a few men in the Secret Service are not in agreement with the President. He knows of them but is not aware of who the individuals are so he takes care not to share too much sensitive information in his policies. They are the good guys. Come on David; let's ski down further so we don't call attention to ourselves. When we get down to that big fir tree on the right, stop and put your hand on your knees and act out of breath. We can stop and talk further. Do you understand what to do? Good let's go," and he pushed off.

David didn't have to fake much being short winded. He managed a weak laugh as he pulled up alongside Jim.

"Jim I feel overwhelmed by the information. I thought I knew it all," David gasped as he bent forward and rested his hands on his knees.

Jim responded, "That's just the tip of the iceberg. Listen David," Jim grabbed him by his arm. The intense tone made David look up into Jims' face. "Susan is still alive!"

David immediately fell into the snow. It was so apparent that something unusual happened that the two secret service men began to move toward them and the Vice-President signaled that they were okay. "Now David, I realize this is a shock. She's alive and doing fine." David was sobbing and gasping for air. "Get hold of yourself now and listen to me. She is in the Witness Protection Program and being well cared for. The President thinks that is fine because it supposedly distracts them from you. I can arrange for you to see her but realize I can't offer much protection. I suggest that you meet her alone. Be careful David, it's dangerous. Some of the agents believe you are a potential enemy. They don't know what you know except you are involved with the President," Jim warned him.

"Where is she? Oh God," David cried.

"She is up in Canada on the west coast. I'll get you a map and notify the agent who she's with to leave her alone for awhile, but I can't let everyone know. There may be a leak or a double agent in the group. They are back and forth over the entire world and although I trust the majority, caution is the number one priority. Don't get your hopes up David. She was hysterical when we got hold of her. She is convinced you let go of her."

David dropped his head and sobbed, "I did."

"David, David, it's all right. The first step is getting you to Susan, and then we can meet again and make some plans to get out of this mess. Now I'm sure you know you are being watched and monitored, we all are, all the time. Thanks in large part to you. So just be cautious in your choice of words. Remember I'm here and I'm your friend. Thanks for being so direct with me and by the way, congratulations on choosing a different way of life. As you go on, you'll experience a lot of things in a most refreshing new way. Come on, let's go home and get some Thanksgiving dinner."

David spent Friday with the family and then flew back to San Francisco on Saturday. There were two e-mails when he arrived home. The first one was from the President saying he pretty much could do what he pleased until New Year's but that he was expected to be in Washington D.C. for New Year's Eve and Day. That was always a big event for the President and First Lady. They hosted an annual New Year's Ball at the White House and New

Year's Day was always reserved for celebrating new decisions and promotions. That group consisted of friends and business associates. It was a black tie affair and often an entertainer or two was included. This year there would be a couple of diplomats as well.

The second e-mail was from Jim and Carol. They again expressed their enjoyment of his company and wrote that Jim made sure of David's schedule and requested that he go to Washington State. The purpose of the trip was to check on property for the President and then go up into Canada for some type of special salmon that Carol wanted for her Washington Christmas Party. If David wanted to, he could stay with them in their Washington D.C. condo for the upcoming events. David was elated; he hadn't expected the Vice-President to move so fast. He did notice however, that there was caution written between the lines of this email.

***

David spent the next few days enjoying being at home in California. He did some yard work, shopped, paid bills, and spent time with Grace and Chris Brown. One weekend he invited them over and they barbequed in the backyard. David couldn't remember when he had done this, maybe two years ago. He even took a ride up to the top of Mount Saint Helena and bought a small evergreen tree. He put it up in the house, hoping Susan would enjoy it when he brought her home. He tried to think of possible presents for her. He window shopped in Calistoga and nearby towns for hours. He hadn't taken the time in many years to do this, at last he decided that he might get some better ideas for her when he went to Washington State.

Going to bed that night, he couldn't keep his mind off his wife. He would make things up to her and keep some promises.

David fell asleep smelling and dreaming of her. He was excited to share his new life.

Chapter 18

David left for Washington State intent on traveling into Canada a few days sooner than he planned. He updated his resume and thought perhaps he would check out little mountain towns for possible sales of small local newspaper businesses. David was not missing all the confusion and rushing about in his career. He found it pleasant to think about nothing. He rented a vehicle in case his time got short and he and Susan needed to fly back. He took his time going up north and weaving back and forth between Interstate 5 and Highway 101 as he wished to see this or that sight.

***

Weather was pleasant until he reached Portland, Oregon and the rain began to pound the windshield. One day was almost spent by the time he arrived. He stopped at a roadside inn overlooking the sound, even though he couldn't see it. He could smell the salt water. A thick fog hung over him until he felt like he was totally alone. He slept fitfully and woke with a jump. Sweat beaded down his face and chest, from dreams of being chased.

Frightened, he had no clue who or what was after him. He gasped for air in the hot humid room. He shoved the window open to let in fresh air. Fear overwhelmed him. A panic attack like nothing he'd ever known. "Whew! What was all that about?" His own voice startled him. Shaken, he decided to stay awake. After a long shower, he ordered breakfast brought to his room. By the time he called the realtor in Seattle, Washington to look at the property the President was interested in purchasing, he'd calmed considerably. The appointment was later the following afternoon.

***

David headed north after lunch and amused himself with a Christmas Music disk that Grace gave to him. He sang out loud and laughed at the sheer joy of the season. Like a child, he looked forward to dinner on the Wharf and all the Christmas decorations. He hadn't done that since they left New York. Susan begged him to take her to San Francisco Alioto's for lunch and sightseeing during the holidays, but he was always too busy. San Francisco was exciting during Christmas. Seattle was the same, much to David's delight. He found a golden nutcracker and beautiful diamond cross pendant he hoped Susan would like.

The night air chilled him, so David took a taxi back to his hotel even though he wanted to walk and stretch his legs even more. He hoped the place where he stayed had a small gym and hot tub. He did find an exercise room, however it was full, so he returned to his hotel room. Tucking himself in bed, he picked up the Bible and began to read. He experienced again, the overwhelming fear and began to pray. Before long, while he was still praying, his body relaxed and he felt the calm of the Lord in the room beside him. He relaxed. He realized that the chances of being watched were great. The Vice-President warned him to be careful and that things aren't always what they seem. *Maybe*, he thought, *I've let my guard down too much or maybe I'm expecting too much out of this trip...*

Damp fog greeted him when he left the room the next morning and David met the realtor at noon. He felt uncomfortable with the man's sleazy innuendos. David wasn't in the know about this particular deal for the government. He would find out soon enough, but this guy was annoying the heck out of him.

A well-dressed man, the realtor drove him to the property and asked him a myriad of questions. "What are you planning for this property?"

"I'm only here to walk the area and take pictures. I am gathering information such as acreage, water, sewage, etc. for my boss." He sighed, hoping that the questions would stop. "It's sure long ways out here, how many miles from town would you say? It's forty acres of forest here and the dirt road is terrible."

"I'm just the realtor. I don't know much about this myself as I received the listing only a couple of days ago." He shrugged his shoulders. "I haven't had much time to work this between my other clients."

David remembered some talk last year about a small compound or sanctuary where diplomats could meet on the West Coast. He wasn't surprised that this type of realtor was involved, a real con artist if ever he knew one.

David decided to take a ferry up the coast the day after he checked out the property for the President. He would pick up a vehicle later. He felt traveling by water might be a little safer. He arrived around three o'clock in the afternoon after hiring a small fishing boat to take him to the little town where Susan lived. Jim provided a good map right up to the cabin, so no stops for guidance were necessary.

He saw her first, her back was to him. He was behind a tree and he wouldn't have known her if she'd not walked out of the cabin. He noticed her slight body and a much more pronounced limp. He felt like a school boy as he approached to her. David tried not to startle her as he walked up to the log where she sat. The wolf-malamute animal that came with her gave a low warning growl.

"Susan," he whispered. The striking blue-eyed dog that stood next to her moved her ears forward. An unusual animal that seemed haunting and beautiful with her heavy black and white fur and icy cold stare that watched every move David made toward them.

Susan jumped. Startled she said, "David! What are you doing here? How in the world did you find me?" Frightened by his presence, something in the way she looked at him sent chill bumps down his arms. Her eyes turned dark with anger. "Why are you here?" The shrill of her voice shot through to his heart. The dog hunched in response to her tone, ready to pounce.

David ached to hold her, but both the human and animal's body language indicated touching her was not a good idea.

"Susan," David began again. "Let me talk with you for a few minutes." He started to speak with hesitation. His words hung in the air. Susan listened until he paused.

She stiffened, "David, I'm different, you're different. I did love you so much. Too many things have happened between us. I can't go back." She gulped between sobs. "Brooke said you might show up. I didn't want you to. I won't go. I'm happy here. I'm in good hands. I have good health care. I like the people and my dog. As you can see, I'm no longer in remission. My legs and arms are in terrible pain, although this climate is better for me. The dog helps me up when I fall, or she'll get help. Brooke and I love each other." She looked anxiously around. "Brooke will be here soon. People don't like you."

David took a chance and stepped closer. He lifted her fingers and kissed them. He pulled her close for a hug, and she didn't pull away. He shared with her his testimony, told her how he'd found Jesus and had been forgiven. He asked her forgiveness for the wrong he'd done to her. He continued, "I miss you Susan. I miss you and your beautiful long hair. Please forgive me, let's try again. Come home. I love you with all my heart. I've changed; you've got to believe me honey."

"No David," she shifted. "You let go and pushed me away. How could I ever trust you?"

Susan backed away from him, "I told you, I have someone else. I love her and she loves me. We keep each other happy and satisfied. You must go."

David gasped, "Susan, you can't be serious!"

The sky darkened and Susan pushed him to leave. "You'd better go David. I'm not going with you. I don't trust you. I don't want to. You can keep your Jesus and new life." She waved him away.

David saw tough, raw, beauty. The last rays of a golden sun streamed through the fog that rolled in off the water. She would always be beautiful to him, but she rejected him. She hadn't forgiven him, and he could see she was serious. His heart was broken.

He'd just lost the woman he still loved.

"Come on Gypsy," she called the dog, "it's getting cold." She stood. She pulled her coat tighter about her frail body and made her way up the pebbled path toward the cabin. David followed her with his eyes. The cabin was brightly lit and he could see a Christmas tree inside. This time he allowed tears to roll down his cheeks. He had to let her go again.

She never looked back.

He struggled with the realization that he'd let her go. And now, she'd walked away.

Chapter 19

    David flew out of Seattle to Santa Rosa, California and asked the Browns to pick him up. He took them out for dinner and told them all about the events. They were full of understanding and encouragement. They told him they had noticed subtle changes starting to come through Susan before the accident. They thought maybe it was some of her medication. Also, they mentioned she was lonely and beginning to withdraw.

    The Browns felt the doctor and his wife were a little on the weird side. The couple was almost overprotective at the time. David told them how the good doctor Randall, called him with the news that Susan was alive and wanted to discuss the situation over lunch in the city. David felt a check-mark soon after the police detective assured him it was not possible. David felt the doctor had some devious reason for lying to him about Susan's death.

    Then Chris hopped in the conversation. "I agree things were not what they seemed and something seemed all wrong. The whole story about what happened became messy and mixed-up." He pulled his hand through his hair, "We met the doctor when the detective went to the house. We spoke with the detective and explained that you were in Europe when the doctor and his wife showed up as far as we knew. We were told that they wanted in the house to get Susan's things. Well, the detective wouldn't let either of them in. The detective didn't know who we were." He hung his head and shook it slowly, "That's about all we know, David, except we felt they were pushy people," explained Chris. "Then when you told us that you let her go, I thought maybe there was something strange going on, beyond just the weird indication that someone wasn't telling the truth about her being dead. Who do you believe, you know?"

Grateful, David hugged his friends' good-night, as they dropped him off at his house. "We're sorry David, don't give up on Susan, we are all praying for her. We love you too, now go get some rest." Grace said.

***

David tossed and turned. He woke himself up telling Susan how much he loved her. He closed his eyes again and saw her beautiful dog. Gypsy was fiercely protecting Susan. David fell into a peaceful sleep praying and asking God for help and strength to continue his walk.

The following night David began another night of fitful sleep. He woke every hour. There were several small earth tremors that he attributed to his wake-up calls. At three o'clock with no moonlight, he jumped and woke himself screaming. He had been dreaming of the doctor and the man had an iron grip on his jacket. David tried to get out of his grasp. The struggle caused the grip to become tighter. David reached to grab his hand when all of a sudden he saw the ring on Randall's right hand. The signet ring sent sparks with an eerie glow and seemed to be burning through David's jacket and into his flesh. The pain was so great that after David woke, he looked at his arm where he was amazed to see a fresh burn mark. He thought the mark was very strange as he didn't remember burning himself when he lit the fireplace earlier the day before.

The following day, while raking the back yard, he decided to talk with the Browns. He put on his old college team jacket and there was a large burned hole in the right shoulder sleeve.

"Things are squirrelly and weird around my house lately," he explained to his friends. All three talked at length about the strange events that had been occurring in David's home. Each person told about things that they observed the last several months. A single thing in common that they all noticed was the unusual ring that the good doctor always wore. David added that he noticed a beautiful blue color while Chris and Grace argued that it was a deep ruby red. Then David told them that he had seen the rare ring before on several people, including the President, Vice-President, Chief of Security, one of the top Military Brass, and a couple of foreign diplomats.

Mr. and Mrs. Brown glanced at each other and Chris explained that there could be demonic activity of some sort. The three friends prayed together for protection and then Chris gave David a couple of books to read on the subject.

"You know," David shook his head, "I don't believe all this but boy it seems to be making sense. I feel like we are in some sort of twilight zone."

"Well David, in a sense you are. We do often walk and live in a spiritual realm so we are more sensitive to this type of activity as compared to an average person. Stay for dinner David." Grace warmly invited him. David declined, he was feeling very sleepy. He hugged them both and trudged home through the warm winter season evening. Christmas lights twinkled from windows and roof tops, Christmas trees brightened the neighbor's windows and the air felt close, grey and heavy with fireplace smoke.

After a hot cup of soup, he curled up in his favorite front

room chair by a freshly lit fire. He began reading so intently that he dozed off in the middle of a page. What seemed a long while later, he looked at his watch. The time was late so he reluctantly took himself to bed. The next day, he cleaned and scrubbed the house in preparation of an extended leave to Washington D.C. He planned on spending Christmas with his sister and her family, afterward, he would travel to Washington. Alone, he took down his tree and spent the last evening in Calistoga with Grace and Chris.

He drove himself to San Francisco where he purchased several loaves of sourdough bread to take with him. Because this was business, he flew first class. Finishing up dinner on board, he attempted to sleep. He woke to the airline hostess gently putting a blanket on him. He had been dreaming of Susan's dog Gypsy. The dog's eyes were brightly shining and she kept pacing back and forth on the path in front of the little cabin. Every so often she would stop and whine turning in a circle. She seemed to be searching for something. All of a sudden she leaped up on the top of a large rock. She threw back her head and the wolf part of her began to cry out. David sat up and rubbed his eyes. "Thanks." He mumbled to the stewardess. He shook as if trying to brush off an unseen enemy.

"You've had quite a difficult time sleeping." She was gently shaking David, "You were talking and crying at the same time. Would you like some water or perhaps a cup of coffee?" The attractive brunette pulled her hair behind her ear and bent down to hear his answer as she whispered.

"No. Thank-you," he replied, feeling badly nauseated and icy cold. He tried to settle back down but the image of the beautiful animal kept appearing in his mind. He looked at his watch and sat up. They would be landing in about thirty minutes which would be ten o'clock p.m. His brother-in-law met him and after the short visit with his sister and her family, he continued on to Washington D.C.

Still, he couldn't shake the vision of Gypsy.

Chapter 20

The Vice-President was unexpectedly in the back seat of the limo that picked David up from the airport. Startled, David immediately began to question him. He put his finger to his lips to quiet David and although Bob was a trusted driver, the sound proof window went up between them. "David, Susan has died. She didn't suffer. We need to decide what you would like to do?" He spoke softly.

David felt deep sorrow, but he also felt relief. Susan had been suffering and now he could totally let go of her with no more guilt plaguing him. "When did it happen?"

Jim spoke, "Two nights ago, about eight p.m. Pacific time."

"Oh," David groaned. "That explains the dream I experienced." He couldn't contain the sob that burst out for his loss, Gypsy's loss, and Susan's salvation. David cried for everything sad that came to his mind. Carol met them at the door and held David tight for a long time and then steered him toward the living room where they prayed for Susan, her family, and then guidance for themselves.

The next few days were full of meetings, luncheons, and

dinner parties, but each morning and evening the two men were able to get away for a short walk in the nearby park.

One bright morning, the Vice-President stumbled. He complained of chest pains so David and Bob took him to his private doctor. A series of tests were ordered. His attending physician said more would be needed to be done in the New Year. There were signs of a slight heart attack in the past, but nothing new or conclusive was showing up now. Jim was reprimanded for not resting enough and allowing too much stress in his life. He joked with the doctor but was not at all convincing. Carol ran down the front steps of the house to meet them with her husbands' robe and slippers insisting that he rest for a couple of days before the New Year's events.

The New Year's Party was as usual, very small and very extravagant. David was called upon to come and stand next to the President. The Commander-in-Chief announced that David was being congratulated and thanked for a good job the past few years. He credited him for getting the world computers in place and connected. He accomplished a major feat in uniting all the countries and getting them into a one-world system. David was also commended for the ways in which he manipulated the public in the United States and abroad. He made things easy and palatable for the public to follow the will of their leaders. Transitions were all in all, quite smooth with few glitches. He received a standing ovation from his peers as he received a very special gift, a ring that matched the President's and his peers. "This ring has been reserved for you for sometime David," the President explained. "You have earned it with our heartfelt thanks." The Russian leader received one as well. After the ceremony, both David and the Russian were advised behind closed doors what power the rings held.

David was astounded at its capabilities. He could control several things with a laser beam. A gentle flick of his finger was all it took to set the laser beam off. It was also programmed in such a manner that he could talk with any one of the ring bearers or have conference calls. Little did he know that one day he could be under its power as well? From the moment the ring had been slipped on his finger, he began to have doubts that he made the right decisions in the past. He also began to have confused feelings.

Chapter 21

David returned from Europe a week later to Calistoga. He had been so busy between meetings and conference calls; that he hadn't spent much time dealing with his personal life. Now for the most part, he wanted quiet and time to think. He needed to grieve. He left a message for the Browns that he was taking the phone off the hook and would get in touch later.

Susan's presence was everywhere. He could smell her warm body and he could feel her soft hair brushing against his face. With his eyes squeezed shut, he tried to see her smile again, free from pain and full of love for him. He opened their closet and reached in for her blue dress hoping it could somehow help him with her image. Grabbing her pillow, he buried his face and inhaled, there it was, her lavender scent reached deep into his senses. "Oh Susan," he moaned. "Now I haven't anyone."

David couldn't bear to get into bed. He opted for their favorite blanket and curling up on the sofa with a warm fire softly burning out, he didn't remember falling asleep.

***

He heard the sound of his name being called out it woke David with a start. Rubbing his eyes, he looked at the clock and saw that it was three o'clock in the morning. "David!" He sat up and looked around the room. It was bright and full of sunlight. He thought to himself that it was odd for it to be so light this time of year. The fireplace held a couple of remaining embers. "David!" The voice insisted, demanding, harsh, and loving all at the same time. David gasped. He wondered if this was what people were talking about when the Voice of the Lord spoke. No one stepped inside his home while he slept, yet this was audible and he was awake. Any other circumstance would have made his hair stand on end. Yet...this voice contained a calming effect. David stuttered, "I don't know if this is you Lord, forgive me, I haven't paid much attention to you in quite awhile. Help me. I don't understand. If this is you, then tell me what you want."

"Susan is gone David, she's fine. She is well and just as my Word promises, no more tears and no more pain. I want you to get hold of your sister-in-law and Mrs. Brown. Ask them to help you disperse her things. Give them to charity. You and Mister Brown put your house in Calistoga in order. It's to be used for people needing help. Tell Chris and Grace that they will know what to do." The Voice paused, and then continued. "Fear not, my son, I have chosen you for a purpose. I need you now in the Middle-East. I will direct your every step. Keep reading in the Word and listen to my voice. Don't look to the right or left. Stay with your job and I will tell you when to resign."

David was overwhelmed as he managed to mutter, "Okay." He fell into a deep sleep. Four hours later, he woke refreshed with an urgent sense of purpose. His acceleration was unlike anything he felt since boyhood.

He began to get his home in order, spoke with the Browns,

had a lot of prayer and fasting time, and tried to read as much as possible in the Word. The remaining two weeks in Calistoga went by quickly.

Chapter 22

Winter snow covered the mountains, the prairies, David watched as the crop circles of Kansas and the Great Lakes came into view, and passed. In New York he received a briefing by White House correspondents and then a small group scheduled travel to a remote area unknown to any of them until they winged their way across the ocean.

David was amazed at the smooth transition back in California. He left the two vehicles behind for anyone to use. He took care of everything and put his house in order including updating his will. He paid his insurance a year in advance. The Browns assured him they would watch over everything and use his belongings as directed. He marveled at their calm spirit and willingness to do what was requested. David asked for prayer before he left. He also called the Vice-President on a pay phone from the San Francisco airport. Airport security was getting tighter. David understood that the public had a need for greater security and peace of mind.

The bombing at New York World Trade Center on September 11, 2001 changed the people of the world forever.

David was surprised at how calm he was. God seemed to be all around him. He felt as if he were in a time warp, where he was outside himself watching the action take place in slow motion. Like a fish in a net, he was caught in the spirit world listening very carefully. It felt surreal, a favorite term going around soon after the bombing. He seemed keenly aware of his surroundings at all times and his intuitive senses were heightened and finely tuned. He laughed to himself. *This must be the feeling mothers have when they tell us they have eyes in the back of their heads.*

The desire for alcohol and tobacco was gone with no after affects and he slept as well as any ten year old boy after a long day in the forest. He had an insatiable appetite for Bible reading and was continually amazed at the parallels pointing to current world events. David saw a huge crack in the average American way of life. The people were beginning to struggle financially at an individual level. The world as a whole grew increasingly uncomfortable. He could understand where it would soon be less difficult to convince American citizens to give up more civil rights, join a world banking system, accept a mark on their flesh, become more involved with the United Nations and give up their weapons. *Poor people*. He thought to himself. *They are so very busy working hard to make a living, they aren't living.* Much to his surprise, he realized he was coming out of the same way of life and he was alive now more than ever.

One day, he had thought, it would be nice to take the train or bus clear across this big beautiful United States of America. He had realized as he stood on top of Pikes Peak, when he visited Colorado years before, the majestic power of his great nation. People rallied together as never before but he was afraid it would be short-lived.

One of the major elements of change his group discussed was fear. The fear factor was an important element in manipulating an unsuspecting public. David noticed that fear around the world had grown much greater. Some people could smell it on each other.

David could almost hear negative leaders sighing with a breath of relief that terrorists dealt a terrible blow to the economy, pushing the United States closer to a world banking system. Terrorist incidents made their job easier and they didn't have to be the bad guys.

Then a sobering thought came to light, David was one of them, committed to a cause of world unity but then that meant death to each individual nation, culture, individuality of humans, and certain inalienable freedoms. Was it really so good? Or was this a fallacy? He surmised that one needed to take a hard look at all the angles. He sensed that he wasn't crazy but sane even as he was running from an insane world. The Bible promised that Gods' people are of a sound mind. David began to think more and more in realms of black and white. Yes, he was a Christian, a true believer and soon he realized he would be kicking off an agenda that was building a strong opposition such as the world has not yet seen. The opposition against Christianity was so strong that fear and dread were permeating everyone. Shaking as if to brush off unseen demons, David began to pray and fast that God would be merciful toward the people that believed in Jesus Christ.

David found it harder and harder to communicate with his co-workers. He did more listening than speaking. "Soon," he thought out loud. "I'm going to have to quit this job." The Lord was already preparing him for the transition.

His flight across the ocean seemed long but it gave David some time to think. The New York meeting was two days during which they toured the devastation of the two World Towers. They took an assignment of where each company involved was financially, especially the banks. There was definitely a domino effect in process. Many small banking systems had already gone under during the past ten to twenty years. Now larger ones were feeling the effects. The situation was escalating faster than the average citizen realized.

David worked more in Europe than back in the States. He had loved the travel and excitement along with the night life when he could take Susan with him. Meetings were one after another, first with the country's dignitaries, then the bankers and CEOs of large corporations. Occasionally, a small corporation would be approached if there were some type of arrests; otherwise, they would go broke on their own without any merger help.

Chapter 23

John Edwards sat straight up in bed and rubbed his eyes. Small built with sandy-hair, he shook his head. He turned toward his clock. It flashed neon-green which indicated, one o'clock a.m. John blinked and felt startled as he looked around the lit room. Three angels surrounded his bed and each held a flaming sword. They were medium built with blond hair and piercing brown eyes. The room was not bright but intense; the swords moved in circles around the angels, pushing strange forms away from him.

A soft voice filled the room, "You are a beloved son John, a willing and faithful servant of mine. I have a special call for you. It is hard but do not fear, I have you prepared well for what you are to do," the audible voice of God spoke through one of them.

John immediately fell to his knees in bed and covering his face he began to worship. "Praise you almighty Lord. I am willing. Please just make it clear to me what it is you would have me to do. Give me strength in what it is so that I am successful. Open my ears to listen so that I can obey."

God spoke, "Look into your mind and memories, remember the past so that you might be strengthened for the future." John began to remember.

***

A little boy stood in the pouring rain outside Macy's Department Store. The store was in a large city, but he couldn't remember where. It was Christmas Eve and he was lost. People rushed back and forth and past him on the sidewalk. John was pushed aside and stumbled as someone tried to hail down a taxi. They were last minute shoppers. No one noticed the tiny piece of humanity. He was knocked down. Three forms with huge wings picked him up. They were white beings with golden ropes wrapped around their robes. "I cannot go with you, you are strangers, my mother told me," the boy spoke. "Well child," one of beings sighed lovingly, "Sleep then." The next thing John remembered was standing next to his mother in the ladies dressing room in another department store. She was on her knees weeping and begging God to find her son. "Oh where have you been?" She cried as he held him tight. Little John had been pushed outside by a greedy crowd as he and his mother stood near the door. She let go of his hand for a split second to check the price of a tie for his father.

John saw these beings many times thereafter. They came to his wedding and each of his children's births. They were there again the night of a terrible accident. He was driving in the rain when he lost control of their family vehicle. Plunging over a bridge in South America, his van landed upside down. He could not save his family but he saw the angels with them as he stumbled out of the water and out of breath. Many came to know Jesus because of the accident; the missionary family was a much loved part of the community.

The angels appeared again years later at his parents' funeral. Succumbing to a fire in their home; his dear godly parents went to be with their Creator.

This time the beings spoke to John. Their voices spoke in unison, like twin thoughts. The tone was gentle and musical. "Fear not John. We are with you always. God has seen and cries with you. He sends us to tell you nothing is in vain. Everything happens for a reason for the good of God's children." John could no longer control the tears that ran down his face; he cried out to them that he was alone. "No, never," they chimed back. "You have many loving brothers and sisters in Christ. They are all over the world. Many pray and intercede for your well-being."

As John learned what community living in God was and allowed his congregation to love and care for him, he began to heal from past hurts. Many hurts came from well meaning people in the Church and some from wolves in sheep's clothing as well.

Apart from preaching The Word of God, Johns' favorite pastime was sharing food and gospel together in someone's home. Little by little, as the years passed by-between a Word of the Lord through someone, the scriptures, and prayer time, John learned of his new direction. He walked with Jesus and heard His voice as far back as he could remember.

***

One day, John began to feel restlessness in his soul. It was a soft quiet autumn morning where a brisk wind swirled colored leaves around his feet as he walked along a historical path. He found himself among the red rocks of Garden of the Gods. Large rock and cliffs of red sandstone began to glow a bright gold color as the sun rose and hit them. An unusual silence stopped the breeze and singing wildlife. The small man sensed something wasn't finished in his life yet. He was in his late fifties and couldn't shake this drawing away from his congregation. The feeling was like when he was first called into ministry and then on to missionary work. He looked around and began to seek the Lord earnestly. He continued to walk in the quiet air, observing the morning star and sunrise. He loved living under the shadow of Pikes Peak. He never got enough of constant color changes in the morning sky and the red rocks. It was breath-taking against the eastern slope of the Rocky Mountains. He remembered overwhelming emotion as he approached the mountains by car after a long hot summer out on the plains. John grew up in the area and he missed being in the tall green pine and fir trees.

A humble preacher, he began to pray for clear direction for the future. As God answered and things began to fall into place, John realized he was ready and at peace with where God was sending him. On one occasion, he asked God if he were to have a companion and who it might be.

A member of his congregation called when he returned home to share with him that while he and his wife were in prayer, the name David kept repeating itself. He wondered if John might understand. John laughed out loud and reassured his hesitant brother that it made a tremendous amount of sense!

John called his flock together later in the week to share with them that God was calling him to Jerusalem. He told them he was to meet a David there and to listen for more of God's divine plan. He was told that he could not look to the right or left but to leave within the week. John asked for prayer and support. Many people stood up to encourage him, adding that they had seen a vision of him there in the middle of the streets of Jerusalem. Many were praying and fasting for John. The elders agreed to keep the congregation together until he returned. They all decided they could support this vision for at least a year.

Chapter 24

Thunder rumbled and lightning flashed as John's plane landed in New York City. Between the pelting rain, baggage checks and security problems at various terminals, the trip was three times as long as it would have been a scant twenty years earlier. Although John purchased a cheaper flight, his church body insisted on sending him first-class. "Only the best for a King's Kid," they all agreed.

John laid back his head and day dreamed as the engines roared below. Flying through the clouds triggered memories as different shapes floated past. He was amazed at how quickly his life had gone. "Kind of like the twinkling of an eye," he laughed. He considered the vapor that he knew as his life. His world moved progressively forward, but humanity spiraled in the opposite direction. Humans, so technical in scientific advancements, especially in the fifties and sixties, moved faster and faster at warp speeds toward the future. However, their spiritual condition grew seemingly worse, similar to the Dark Ages.

Never had John counseled so many people in false gods and beliefs. He discussed this with other Christian leaders and they all experienced a decline of human behavior. He remembered scriptures pointing to this very thing near the end of the age. Worship of man and different idols were the worst. The fall of Rome was due to the decline of human values and unhealthy desires for same sex relationships. John noticed that the people in the United States worked so hard to keep their jobs and pay their bills that they had no time for family and friends. Most people were so involved in their work places that they came home to take the phone off the hook and go to the television or internet. Worse still, cell phones offered affordable instant communication and children demanded to have their own to carry around. People lost themselves in unreality. Life wasn't demanding if you didn't have to respond. As a result, they began to depend more and more on Big Brother Government to step in and take care of things for them in their daily lives.

John connected world changes with warnings in the Bible. He often pointed out events and current happenings to warn his congregation. He became more involved with community living and encouraged families to spend more quality time together. A short five minutes of quality time was not enough. So many parents believed that if they spent a few positive minutes each day with their children, it was better for them than paying no attention at all. As a result, the parents were able to justify leaving their children alone most of the day. That way both parents could work and be able to leave some of the most important decision making to teachers. Thoughts never occurred to them that children always need someone to help, or just be there as they learn the lessons of life. If parents were not around, then someone else would be answering and teaching their youngsters. Unfortunately the teachers came from televisions, computers, and public school systems. Most examples of being a good person were humanistic beliefs based on social justice, a concept created by the government to perpetuate politically correctness in the community.

A big deception occurred near the end of the twentieth century and beginning of the twenty-first century with the false interpretation of scripture which made everything even worse. People, leaders in various churches argued about what was right and wrong. In some Bible translations, God warned that in the end, people would say, "Right is wrong and wrong is right." Truth became watered down and re-invented. God was being taught as mother instead of father. He could be unisex; therefore since sex was made by God then all could enjoy one another as a gift from God. Children were inconvenient, disliked as were older folks. Older citizens became a burden to society and interfered with one's working and social lives. Besides that, they were expensive to support. If they couldn't work, they were of no use materially to society or the tax structure. As a result, there were many legal ways in place to get rid of them. Who needed history when computers were instant encyclopedias?

John mulled fast moving thoughts as he remembered some outstanding changes in his world as he grew up. "Values Clarification" was a new modern class in the late 1960s and early 1970s in college. John was required to take the course for one of his socialization programs. Although he attended a Bible believing and Bible accepting college as a young man, many questionable classes were required for graduation. This popular class was the "in" thing because scholars believed that graduating children weren't well equipped to be on their own and taking care of themselves and society as a whole. As a result, most companies on the cusp of innovation and technology forced their employees to take these types of classes under one guise or another. Personnel Departments changed their names to be the Human Resources Departments in many companies. A myriad of confusion grew as companies merged their departments under one totality. Employees felt no one would help them if they had a problem they couldn't discuss with their boss.

John learned from his congregation about the bar code and what it could do. He wanted to learn to integrate a computer system for his bookkeeping in the church. The more he learned, the more he realized how little he knew. He took computer classes at the local junior college some years after he graduated only to find that as fast as he learned, new changes and upgrades took over. He could hardly keep up. One form of teaching contradicted another. People refused to take responsibility for their behavior. Blame and accusations resulted in no accountability and any problems were someone else's fault.

The preacher had a judge in his congregation that came to him for prayer. He wanted to step-down before retirement because he was so frustrated with changes to laws in the United States. He told John the legal system was moving backwards. Children were taught that they could make their own decisions, it didn't matter what their parents or elders thought or believed. Their input wasn't important. As long as they hurt no one, they were free to do what they wanted. The children had no idea of the hurts they were inflicting on those who loved them. Some countries taught hatred of their elders and found ways to euthanize the elderly. God's Word calls it murder. The whole issue of abortion was in a constant argument. No one cared what God (if there was one), taught about what matters in life. It was a popular belief that ancient history and the cultures back then were uncivilized. Yes, the world traveled a path of self-destruction.

But why were so many people not seeing all these strange signs and wonders? God warned the world in the Bible that many were blinded in spirit and truth. Many people had itching ears and wanted to hear what was good. He laughed to himself; he remembered a cat he once owned. He was so concerned she couldn't hear that he took her to the vet. The doctor told him that she was fine, but enjoyed selective hearing. She only heard him when she chose to!

One thing glared out in John's mind, the speed and ability of the satellites. A person could instantly bring information into his home, office, or any place in the world. Changes were constantly updated. One could press a button and begin to see and speak with a communications reporter assigned to a given satellite. Somewhat like a chat-room on the internet except now you could go and sit down with other people in that room in your own living room.

John sighed; he wondered if he were just getting old and tired. He thought that maybe he didn't want to keep up and learn any longer. He wondered if all older people felt that way, maybe that thought made it easier for them to let their spirits go to a higher place. He began to read the Book of Revelations. The last book of the Bible told him of past and present things to come. As John read, he began to drift off to sleep. He felt as if he were being pulled out of his body. He met the Lord somewhere out in the clouds high in the sky. The three angels were there.

As he looked at the passing plane alongside of him, he questioned, "Am I dead?"

"No, I have plans for you," the Father answered. "I want you to keep your eyes on me and I will tell you what to do. You shall not fear. I am with you. My angels will stay with you as well. I shall call you home in three and one-half years."

John woke as his plane thumped onto the runway. It was late night as he worked his way through the crowded airport and to downtown. He found the hotel where he made earlier reservations and after a snack, he went to bed. Rising with the sun, he showered and dressed for the day. Outside, for a walk and a bite to eat, he waited further instructions.

Chapter 25

David just found out his secret destination. He was on his way to Israel to work on some negative news about the influx of Jewish people coming from around the world. He thought of where he came from and where God was taking him. One thing for sure, he wasn't going to do a news piece. God already told him that he would show him what to do as soon as he landed. He thought of what he had done.

David was a member of an elite team under the guise of war correspondents. He could be sent around the world to scope out the financial status and help different countries get started and hooked into the system. White House correspondents kept them up to date on the various aspects of whom, what, and where. David was good at explaining the one world money system and negotiating while others were writing up reports and two on the team were geniuses at implementing the computer equipment to reach goals set by One World Government or OWG.

David felt impressed by one fellow named Frank Collins, a computer geek who could trouble shoot and correct mistakes unbelievably fast. He could figure out what was wrong with machines just by listening to them. The man was constantly changing programs in corporations, appraising and updating them, bringing each one closer and closer to becoming compatible to each other and the banks.

David's job was to convince the CEOs to accept change as being inevitable. "Better do it now while it is cheaper than later." The leader spoke with confidence. The team told each individual that everyone else was doing it so they needed to or they would fall behind progress. Once in awhile an entrepreneur would argue and begin to start problems. When David could not convince them any further, he would turn the problem over to a corrupt court system. Courts would, of course, rule against the company and levy them so that they would be broken into smaller pieces or financially ruined. As soon as everything was up and running, Frank would change the programs. The lesson was two-fold; it caused confusion and got rid of the older experienced worker. Getting rid of the older experienced people was a good idea. One of the most popular methods was...early retirement. Give the workers an incentive package; it was cheaper in the larger scheme of things. David's team was instructed to look for company dissenters. Age and experience were not good in today's fast growing technical world. The teams were to be subtle in their reporting to the Human Resource departments.

Most of David's co-workers were either divorced or enjoyed several ladies around the world. Moral decay was at an all time high around the globe. A great number of their female acquaintances were young, international stewardesses who had no home to go to, so the arrangement was equitable to all involved.

David was getting tired as they landed in Israel. He declined an invitation to dinner with a co-worker and a French stewardess.

Retiring, he ordered dinner in and planned to take a hot shower after dinner. He gave the bell-boy a tip, flipped on the television, and sat down to a good meal brought by room service. There weren't many programs so he changed the channel to the evening news only to find out that the United States citizens lost their "right to bear arms." The changes became so subtle and sly that people didn't realize what happened until it was too late. David sighed and rubbed his forehead. The country was going to go down easier than one could imagine. There would be militia groups that were scary in many ways. There would be a lot of innocent people hurt in the name of justice. People were being brainwashed in the wrong way. David fell to his knees and prayed, weeping for the people of Israel and Christian brothers and sisters. He knew that now he must quit his job and warn people of impending disaster. It was time and he felt an overwhelming sense of peace.

God's timing was perfect.

All of a sudden a voice he hadn't heard in a long time spoke, "You are crazy. You've flipped your lid this time David. People will never listen to you. A burned-out old man is all you are. You are a worm with no one who cares," the voice sniveled. "Why don't you get a grip on yourself and get a life? That French stewardess has an unattached roommate. Go relax and meet your friend with the girls. A nice glass of champagne will be good for you!" The male voice laughed a loud raucous laugh.

David threw his hands over his ears and screamed, "No! You are wrong! Get behind me Satan. As a matter of fact, I bind you in the name of Jesus Christ and throw you at His feet. Do what you will Jesus," he cried. Then David fought to get up. Frightened, he drank water and anointed himself with oil from a small vial that he carried with him and went to bed. Twice he was awakened. He got into another argument with his enemy. A second time he was being comforted and loved by the Savior. He knew what to do and where to go. He also knew what was going to take place in the days to come.

***

Waking refreshed, David showered and shaved. He poured a cup of coffee from a freshly brewed pot in his room and turned on the morning news, it wasn't much different except that security increased in various parts of the country and around the world.

David pushed through the heavy front glass doors of his hotel and stepped out into the bright morning, Fresh air hit him and he inhaled a deep breath and began his walk down the street. The day was peaceful and the usual market bustle was beginning. He seemed to know exactly where he was going and headed in the direction that he felt led. An urgent, exciting, feeling overwhelmed him as he sensed he was exactly where he should be at this moment of his life.

"Good morning John," David reached out his hand casually as he sat down across from the man that he felt led to. Jesus told him who to look for and his new friend's name. John had been directed likewise.

John reached across the table and the handshake turned into a bear hug. John replied, "It's wonderful to see you David. Jesus told me to come and wait for you. Boy it demanded a lot of trust. I got the congregation to pray for us and to help finance me. I had no idea how to reach you. Jesus told me you would come to this place this morning and then we should go from here."

Both men were surprised yet relieved to see each other. John had never been overseas. He had committed himself to Christ as a small boy and had a passion for what the Bible had to say about future events. Both men spent the day together sharing what they had been learning and the directions they had been given. They entertained what they thought God was leading them to do as a team. As they shared, they were delighted to realize that they were both in agreement about what God had been directing each to do.

John brought David up to date on what was happening in the United States. Some of the militia groups and Veterans were putting up a fight to give up their firearms and the latest scare was biological warfare. Some birds and fish mysteriously died. Experts couldn't tell if the problems were from experiments back in the 1950s or new strains coming from other countries. David was confused, "What do you mean, with all our scientists at work, why can't they figure out the problem?"

"There's a simple answer," John replied. "These darn bugs are mutating faster than we can change antibiotics."

"Wonder why I didn't know that?" David thought out loud. Then he laughed, "Of course, another fear tactic." He had been too busy and naturally the situation was downplayed by the "experts." He mused to himself.

"John, what has God told you?" David questioned him. "I wonder if we have the same information. You have a much better understanding of the Bible so maybe you can clarify things."

"Well, I sure hope so too, because I have scriptures all over in my mind and I know God has us here for a purpose. He also is not the author of confusion. So...let's see where we are going." He grinned and slapped John on the back. "I suggest we pray and share together..."

They realized they were the two prophets God spoke to his people about in the Bible and that their mission was to go out into the streets warning every one of His imminent return. They were to be killed because the people feared them so much and their presence would cause many to be uncomfortable in their guilt-ridden spirits. The men were not afraid because just as prophets before them, had risen, they would also. After dying, it would be after three and one half days that Jesus would come for them. The citizens of the world would become so relieved and excited that these men were out of their lives, that they would exchange gifts and presents with one another. The entire scene would be televised around the globe. All people great and small would have a chance to repent.

John asked David if he knew who the antichrist would be, or as some called the one world leader, and he shared scriptures describing him.

David said, "Yes! Now the scriptures make it clear. I do

believe I may know who it could be." David frowned. "However we aren't supposed to tell anyone. It could be I'm wrong and that would spell disaster for a lot of people." David told John who he thought the man might be.

"I know." John replied. "I don't understand why I didn't figure the name out myself. It fits the scriptures perfectly."

Neither man noticed the ring on David's finger. It was rapidly switching colors and sending small sparks out of the center.

John began to share with David that they needed to find a group of Christians that God had called together and prepared as a nurturing body for them. They needed prayer and strength for the task before them. The two men needed to be anointed with oil and encouraged that they indeed were in the will of God. They also needed help in putting the pieces of this awesome puzzle together.

"Yes," David agreed. Then to his surprise he said, "They're waiting for us at the caves."

Neither man knew the day or time but as soon as they met with the group of believers, Gods' plan unfolded. They had been fasting and praying so they were prepared with food and oils when the two brothers arrived.

Afternoon turned hot and dusty as the men began to share with the small group of believers. The newcomers were astonished at some of the stories that were told. Much suffering had taken place around the world among God's people. David realized that for too long he had been protected and was very ignorant apart from his own little world of journalism and his own political agenda. He remembered a scripture he recently read about having mercy because the world would become so vile that the people would faint from fear and torment. World population would become suicidal. The last few years, David had been busy with settling up the world money system. He hadn't realized how desperate things became. Until now, everything was just stories and other people's problems. Only status-quo was another trite expression tossed about by the world elite. David realized people were sorely lacking rounded educations. He always believed that he was a fairly intelligent human with a good education, but he began to see that many felt the same and their education had been in vain. What one knew about his vocation did not mean he understood how other parts of life worked. A person could be over educated in the intellectual sense and not have an understanding of other people's lives and jobs. Wisdom of life in general was minimal. There was no need for spirituality or intuition or sixth sense. Jiminy Cricket was just a children's story, and an old one at that. He was long dead.

David's compassionate heart broke again for the safety of God's people and animals. Soon, his sobbing turned to righteous indignation and then anger.

One of the older men in the group offered David and John each a small mat to sit on. The group gathered around them. They held hands and prayed over them, anointing them with oil.

For seven days and nights, the small group of people fasted, prayed, supped together, and sought the Lord's direction.

Chapter 26

David stated his concern about doing the right things. He was worried that he would say something out of line or that was not from God. He confessed that Christian community living was new to him. What little exposure he experienced with fellow believers was with Chris and Grace Brown and the Vice-President's family. They were all patient in sharing the love of Christ with him. David realized these people were committed to helping the two of them. He could feel much loving power rising within the group as they came together.

There were twelve believers there and each seemed to be sensitive toward the other, in tune with their needs. They complemented one another in their quest for the truth. They were from all over the world. There were only two from Jerusalem. Those two were born and raised in the Jewish Faith, committing their lives to Christ. They were known as born again Jews or as some called them…Completed Jews.

One of the women began to speak, gently touching David's arm, "David, are you aware of water baptism? Please consider doing this for yourself. I invite you to partake in this act of obedience to God."

Eager to do so, he read in the Bible where he needed to experience that act of faith. He asked John to perform the ceremony on him as the little group prayed. When David came up out of the water, a strange thing happened. His ring finger began to glow brightly, angrily, and started flashing, changing colors.

Sparks started to shoot several directions at once, anywhere from six inches to a foot. His friends shouted at him to throw it off. As David flung it into the air above his head, it exploded into tiny particles. The sky lit up like a huge colorful dandelion that the wind blew apart and pieces drifted everywhere. David and his brothers and sisters began to praise and worship the Lord. With singing and shouts, everyone's hands went up into the air, surrendering to the Most High God. A strange sound came from David's being as he was singing and startled, he quickly threw his hand over his mouth. Laughing, the group hugged him. "It's your love language, a gift from God," they explained. He was blessed because he received the Baptism of the Holy Spirit. A gift that was available to everyone but not all receives it unless they want it. They encouraged him to use his new language often, especially to praise and worship. David never felt so free or so deeply loved and accepted.

As the group grew together, praying, fasting, eating, and fellowshipping, David learned along with them. He began to question things he never learned or understood. One day, he asked God and the group, "why?" An answer was given sweetly and simply. God's purpose for his people is to love Him and to praise Him with a thankful heart. They are to become servants of His and allow His love to flow through to others who would come into and be a part of His kingdom. He does not wish that one of His would be left behind. He wants trust in good times and bad times. He wants us to obey His voice and allow Him to build His son Jesus Christ's character in us. He wishes a personal relationship, a friendship to develop. He asks that people care deeply for one another just as He loves us.

"Does your hand hurt?" Debbie asked. A younger woman with short cropped black hair noticed it was badly burned and his finger showed an angry red mark around it. She gently took it between her two smaller hands and prayed, asking Jesus to touch it and heal it. Then she took a step back, thanking and praising the Almighty for hearing her request.

To David's amazement, there was no evidence of any wound or pain. His right hand was back to normal. As the group studied the Bible together, David began to understand more of what God required. If there was a problem, others helped one another in their walk and understanding.

David commented that he felt overwhelmed. After praying for strength for one another, Justin, an older teen, shared that God won't give us more than we can handle through the power of the Holy Spirit, and He would surely show what He wanted done in His perfect timing. Justin came from South America and Africa. Christians there seemed to be getting a crash course in the Word of God. Their understanding and knowledge accelerated and they were open to the moving of the Holy Spirit. "Why don't we see that in other parts of the world?" David asked. Many of the brothers and sisters began to talk all at once. Everyone expressed a different idea.

John threw back his head and laughed. "I know the answer!" he crowed, "It's because we are human. We are subject to our humaneness and frailties, the sin and division. Materialism, competition, and the belief that one group is better than another. Satan doesn't mind if we go to this or that church or believe this or that way about Christ. As a matter of fact, he believes as well. As long as we are focusing on our differences and not Christ, we are distracted from walking in the truth of the entire Word of God. Our responsibility is a personal relationship with His Son Jesus Christ."

John explained further, "There are well meaning people in the world who are in a lot of trouble. Do any of you understand what a cult is?" He picked up a stick and drew a big circle in the sand with a question mark in the center.

Soft spoken Aimee limped over to sit down and join the group. She volunteered and made a good attempt to explain, "Isn't that a belief where some leader takes scriptures out of context and makes a system or church out of it?"

"Yes, good answer." John nodded. "The belief becomes center instead of Jesus. There are many different systems but when one takes that belief and makes a new religion then that group of people can become very dangerous to society. God warns clearly in the Bible about various beliefs and groups. He describes the differences in the Bible."

"That's why I love the Bible so much," Sara smiled. "God gives us directions so we can be in His will and less trouble will happen. It's our roadmap to Heaven."

"Yes, you are exactly right Sara," John replied. "Sisters and brothers imagine how our precious Lord hurts when He sees and hears how much division separates the Body of Christ. Surely Jesus did not die in vain. He died to make us free to choose who we would listen to. What an awesome God we serve. The fatherly gentleman sighed and shook his head. "Now we have come to a place in history where the Scriptures plainly point to His imminent return. Gods' people have been groaning and praying for this upcoming date with God for centuries. All of you in this group were brought together by God for the purpose of caring for us and each other. David and I need all the love you can give us. There is no foolish thing in this group. We all want to sincerely be in God's will. Thus, in our prayers we need to cover one another's humanness and frailties with the love of Jesus. We must help one another warn the world." He stopped abruptly. "Oh my, there I go again, preaching. I'm sorry, I get carried away and you all know

Jesus and what we are here for. Please forgive this outpouring." John wrung his hands.

"Our precious city is being trampled. God wants to reach every soul. He wants everyone to come at His call. The Bible tells us Jesus will return the way He left. He rose; He will come down with a shout in the Eastern sky to call us to Him." Paul laughed. "See John, it's okay, we are all full of preaching this fine day, I would just as soon call this encouraging and each of us ready to move forward in this task. What an awesome time to be living and I believe privileged to be a part of God's plan."

A striking, small, blond, woman with dark brown eyes that glowed almost black, spoke up. Jennifer was tearing up and as she wiped her face, she struggled to add to the conversation. "We must pray together for all to obey and to faint not, even if that means a physical death. We know we are headed for a better place. We must also pray if there are other Christian groups around the world that might be left after the rapture, a remnant that they strengthen and encourage one another. People must understand that a personal relationship is crucial but we also need our God given community of believers." She gasped, "I try not to entertain my feelings too much, but I do become scared sometimes of what I see around me."

James spoke up in agreement. He was a tall rugged fellow who looked like he had just jumped off the movie screen of Indiana Jones.

"If things aren't lining up with the Word, then they need to ask God where to go for support and worship in purity. I encourage you to spread this to your saved and unsaved loved ones." James shook his head and looked down at his toes. He shrugged his shoulders. "The time is short indeed my brothers and sisters." James looked upward and rolled his eyes changing to another subject. "I was in the city today and there are a million reporters with TV crews scurrying around."

Paul agreed. "You can feel the anxiety and terror mounting. It's like a tremendous thunderstorm building up cloud by huge electrical cloud. From my study of the Word we have roughly forty-two months or three and one half years. The Word says the Holy City will be unrestrained and trampled on for that period of time. What's even scarier is if you break it up into days. We have dear ones, only one thousand two hundred sixty days. There is so little time and so very much to do."

Jennifer began to cry again with the heart of Jesus. Compassion for lost souls welled up inside her. "I've come so far," she sobbed. "I'm so blessed and freed from hurt and despair. The only thing I know to do is much prayer and fasting for David and John. I can see hurt and pain for them and the world. I feel the pain as the Gentiles fight the Truth of God. She began to prophesy. "Thus saith the Lord, My people must put on sackcloth, dark and coarse. It will be a sign of mourning and repentance. My servants are full of power from the My Spirit. Your brothers are going ahead of you. They shall spew fire from their mouths. A fire will devour any enemy that comes near. They can shut the sky from rain. They can turn water to blood and strike the earth with any plague they wish and as often as they wish. Oh! There will be a huge earthquake. Many will die. But be encouraged children many will come to me as a result. There will be drought and rain; there will be plagues and pestilence." Jennifer fell to her knees expressing praise and worship, continuing to sob, she prayed aloud that she hadn't spoken out of turn or made mistakes perhaps speaking apart from what Jesus showed her.

Paul and Pauline, twins, gifted from birth in Gods' Holy Word excitedly shared the scriptures in Revelation, Chapter ten and eleven. Pastor John kneeled near Jennifer to hug and encourage her that she was correct and not to worry about what was taking place.

Pauline spoke first. "Yes fellow travelers, our Bible tells us of all these things. We must not allow discouragement to overtake this calling. There will be seven thousand to die from a huge earthquake coming, a tenth of the city."

Paul continued for her as twins often do, finishing the other's sentences. "After three and one half days, John and David will rise up from being killed. God will command them up in a cloud and many enemies will witness this." Paul raised his hands into the air.

"Let's see," Pauline added. "There are approximately seventy thousand people living in the outer court in Jerusalem. So probably seven thousand will die but wait! Seven thousand will turn to God and give glory to God. They will be terrified with the realization that Christ, not antichrist is the true Lord of all. The Bible says the second woe has passed. A third woe is coming soon."

John was so humbled by the operation of the gifts of the Holy Spirit that tears slipped out of his eye as well. Never had he been in such a well meaning group of genuine believers who were willing to let God operate through them so bravely and lovingly. The flow and cooperation towards a joint work in Christ was remarkable.

Everyone present was important and needed for the message of salvation. David joined in weeping and repentance. He'd never experienced the fullness of God's grace in such a way. "I'm not ready, nor am I worthy," David cried out to his Creator.

John put his arm around David and gathered the group close to lay hands on him. "No one is, David; but like it or not, here you are. No one is worthy; all have sinned and fallen short. But, by God's grace all things work together for good to them that love the Lord. Now, we'll lift each other in love, through Christ Jesus."

John prayed like he had never prayed before as he earnestly prayed for his fellow followers. "Father, we come to you for strength, mercy, and grace. Please forgive us of any sins that have come between us, known and unknown. Help us to listen to your will and direction. Use us for your glory. Give us courage, boldness, and seasoned with sincere humbleness. Please protect us so that we may do your will. Thank-you Father in the Name of Jesus Christ."

Their seventh night was over. No one left the caves. A time came to begin to go to work and listen for the Seventh Trumpet. Believers gathered and put aside water and food for the past seven days and nights but now each returned to their homes. The plan included a rotation basis to make sure there was always a prayer partner night and day at the caves. Who would go at what time would be at the Lord's direction.

***

John and David headed back to the hotel. John's room was paid for in advance for two weeks by his congregation and miracle of miracles; it contained two queen sized beds so David spent the night there because his room was paid for a week. They showered, shaved and laid out their new sackcloth clothing. They went out for a good meal and enjoyed watching the Jewish culture round about them. They did not know the exact time when they were to start preaching but both felt first thing in the morning was a good time.

"Oh my, God! John! You've got to come in here quick!" John dropped his toothbrush and with a mouth foaming full of toothpaste, ran into the living-room study where David tuned in the evening news.

"Look." David shook as he pointed at the unbelievable pictures. People were missing everywhere around the world. The pictures and scenes were dramatic. Vehicles were driverless, planes were on autopilot. David sat on the edge of the sofa; he could hardly breathe, wide blue eyes glued to the picture tube. "I can't believe it, it has really happened. I could give you a zillion worldly excuses for this happening. There are natural disasters and scientific reasons, but now that I know God, I know better," exclaimed David. According to the news sources this strange occurrence took place three days before; while they were praying at the caves.

"That explains why I couldn't get hold of my assistant pastor," John said.

"Oh no, I have to try and reach the Browns right now," David ran his fingers though his hair and frowned. There was a wire for him when he arrived back at the hotel earlier. The couple left a note with money from his assets. They wrote that they knew what he asked of them but God superseded telling them to send everything left to him and to give everything else away. David mourned for his loss but also for their gain. He knew he would see them in three and one half years.

David took a breath and turned to look at his new friend. "Hey buddy, you okay?" "I left no loved ones when I came. I'm fine David and you will be too." John spoke quietly. "Tomorrow is a new day and a big one we must get rest. Let us pray."

David slept hard. The only dreams he had all night were of total supernatural love. He was cradled in the arms of Jesus. He told him be of good cheer and soon He would call for David, His beloved child.

"Good morning John, boy did you sleep hard. If it were not for that lump under the covers and snoring, I would have thought that you were gone as well." David grinned as he greeted him. John scratched his head as he emerged from the bathroom and he suggested they order room service for breakfast.

"I am way ahead of you friend," exclaimed David as a knock sounded on the door. The waiter came in and sniffed arrogantly as he noticed the clothing placed on each end of the unmade beds. "Have a blessed day in Jesus!" The two men laughed as they closed the door giving the gentleman a big tip.

"Hmm...smells good," John commented as he raised the warmer lid. "David, why don't we flip on the morning news and see if there are any changes from last night."

As they ate, they began to put together what happened. Never having been to Jerusalem before, John didn't realize the significant increase in business and more than usual praying with chanting. There were also more prostitutes and harsh venders running around the streets. David noticed an unusual amount of newscasters and press all around. He remembered one of his fellow prayer warriors commenting on the unusual number of press as well but it seemed unimportant to him, just another bombing or whatever, in the everyday life of the Middle-East. He shook himself. He couldn't believe that his heart could be so hard. David was able to understand several languages so they switched stations throughout different countries, all the same story. Theories were all over the world as to what happened. There were some strong cults that believed in UFOs returning to gather their followers so that seemed to satisfy many who were questioning. For others though, it was life as usual... *How can I keep my job until the next payday? And...it made no sense to go across country to a memorial or to make arrangements where there was no body.* Many thoughts went through John and David's minds as they dressed for the beginning of the Seventh Trumpet.

Chapter 27

Grace Brown woke with a jump. She was sweating again even though the room was cold and she already kicked off all the bedcovers.

Chris reached across the bed and drew her close. "Grace, wake up. You've been dreaming again. What's wrong?"

She burst into sobs as she shared with Chris how concerned she felt for several people they were praying for. Some seemed to be growing by leaps and bounds and others had either not accepted her testimony or if they did, there seemed to be no change in their lives. The last few days there was such an urgent call in her prayer life for souls, she was afraid people would miss the return of Jesus.

After forty years of marriage, Chris loved her even more than ever. Lately though, her usual, gentle, and compassionate spirit became impatient with those around her. She would snap at someone or something and then burst into tears begging forgiveness for being so short with them. Chris tried to get her to the doctor believing that hormonal changes were the problem. Grace insisted she was all done with the change of life and this was a different feeling. A strong need for intercessory prayer for all the people in their lives was great. She sensed that her Lord would appear at any moment. She found herself watching and looking in the morning eastern sky. She was feeling stress as never before that she wouldn't have everything in order. Grace knew better but was worried that she and Chris had done everything right in handling the overwhelming job that David left them.

Blessings were so great in the couple's lives that they were speechless with gratitude. God began showing Chris and Grace who David was and his purpose in the scriptures. Their weather in Napa Valley, California was miserable and many grape vines succumbed to the intense heat. With freezing nights and scorching hot days, people flocked to the beach. The people believed in global warning when it fact, just the opposite was happening.

Grace needed encouragement every day from Chris. He felt this was strange as the first twenty years or so of marriage, it seemed she was always the strong positive balance in their walk with Jesus.

Recently, she expressed fear and self-doubt. Grace didn't want to miss hearing from the Lord and that maybe everything in her life to this point seemed in vain. She told Chris she felt tired and felt like she had finished life. She entertained no suicidal thoughts, but maybe things were completed and maybe she was finished with her calling or purpose in life.

Grace struggled to explain to Chris what she felt although it wasn't clear to her "Perhaps, God is asking me to come home honey?"

"Oh Grace," Chris soothed her and stroked her short grey hair. "I think a lot of us are being called right now. Time draws near and God is calling all of his servants. Look at all the signs. You have not worked in vain. He knows your heart Grace. Be strong sweetie, it won't be long. Whether we are here or not, God will take care of those we've been praying for. I understand many seem like children to you. We've known some since they were small."

He held his wife and kissed her forehead. "Come on honey, let's pray together." And they fell asleep in each other's arms.

Chris dreamed of the first time he saw his precious wife. They were working with the Peace Corp in the Holy Land when they met. She was a devout Catholic and he Episcopalian. He believed she was the most beautiful person he had ever met, inside and out.

As their lives together grew, they began reading and practicing living the direction that the Bible gave them. They embraced everyone who would listen to their testimonies. Many people loved the couple, but…many others were uncomfortable and irritated with them. Some disliked their frankness as well.

The couple prayed for Lucky who was returned to her original trainer because of her age. They prayed for their loved and lost ones and then fell into a peaceful sleep.

The daybreak found the childless couple gone from their crumpled bedding. Neighbors who didn't know them very well, wondered about them when their yard went to seed. They figured that their disappearance was due to a trip to the Holy Land of which they often spoke of often.

Chapter 28

Adele woke earlier than usual. Solar flares caused unbearably hot weather and longer days the past few years. Although Easter time was too soon to begin planting and gardening in far northern Montana, old timers learned to listen to certain seasons.

She was excited to begin her day as she quickly moved through her routine of morning chores. Drinking her coffee, she began prayer time and Bible study. Adele and all of her fellow farmers used to rely on the Farmers' Almanac but that wasn't at all helpful the last few years.

Hmm... she thought to herself and getting up, she let her barking dogs outside. *I must have fallen back asleep.* Early rising sun seemed to be much brighter than when she first sat down and her chickens outside were causing a lot of racket.

"That darn Blackie," Adele said out loud. Her new black lab puppy didn't understand that every animal on the property took good care of each other. He teased them all unmercifully.

Adele put on her big hat and with lots of sunscreen smeared all over her, went outside. "Whew! It is going to be another hot day." she mumbled and stretched her frail arms and legs. She was glad she was an early riser. Her plans were to finish tilling her garden plot and put some new seedlings in tomorrow.

After letting her chickens out of their coop, she trotted down the garden path. She felt a strange presence about her. "Paul Lawrence," she raised an eyebrow and spun around. "Is that you?" Paul Lawrence, her husband had been gone many years. Lately though, Adele was missing him. He loved being a gentleman farmer and owning this property. She never thought she would ever get over his young death. It was only a few years after they purchased their dream property. She refused to leave. The thin woman involved herself in church enjoyed God's provisions. So time healed her loss. Her children came often and she was content.

Her fellow worshippers and she noticed that they were all dealing with restlessness in their souls and couldn't quite put their thoughts together.

Adele, still uneasy, began digging a little furrow trying to concentrate on her work. A huge bolt of lightning struck a big evergreen tree at the other end of her garden, causing her to look up. There was Jesus with Paul Lawrence and her children. Jesus reached for her, calling to her to come up into His arms.

She looked down as her body rose up and to her amazement, there were people all around her, some lower, some higher, but all moving into the light. Her soul rejoiced and she joined in the singing!

Chapter 29

Jim Lewis begged Jesus to take him out of the Vice-Presidency. His job had been long and hard. Two terms were more than enough for one person. The Laws changed in the United States now that the New World Order was settled in place and he was only a puppet. His position was in a name and frankly, that did not bother the Vice-President any more. He asked the Lord to take him out of the political scene three years earlier. He was promised by the President after things were in place, he could retire. The President planned to move David into the new position. Jim and Carol knew that was not going to happen. Shortly before David quit, God showed them through an unexpected revelation of circumstances that the Word is always timely, no matter what people try to do to change things. It happened one evening at a Bible study. As the leader began to explain about the witnesses in the Book of Revelation, Jim and Carol instantly knew why David was called to the Holy Land.

Jim knew he would be out of office soon now because no voting for offices existed. A select committee appointed people to fill the chairs. Jim rubbed too many people the wrong way, especially in defense of the rag-tag Christians left around the world. Christians couldn't seem to get their act together on any one issue. They were continually fighting and arguing about one another's denominations, over 5,000 Christian denominations were in place by the early 2000s. After the United States lost Sovereignty to a supreme world leader, the Christian movement seemed to go underground. The small numbers that spoke out were irritants to most rational people. Once again as in past world history, there was only a remnant of Jews around the world. There were few left in North America, most fled to their homeland, which was in ruins. If a person wanted to know about the Jewish faith he could always try to find information on the computer.

Jim sighed as he lay down on the extra-long leather sofa in his office. He punched a call button to his secretary requesting that she not put any calls through for the next fifteen to twenty minutes. His scheduled week was full and a little cat nap was a good idea.

He moaned in pain as he tried to find a comfortable position to settle the heartburn that felt like a mule kicking inside his stomach. He admitted it might have been a good thing to accept Carol's offer to prepare him a sack lunch in the future. He often wondered what he would do without Carol. She was such a helpmate to him. He smiled to himself as he remembered meeting her. She was a high energy, tiny person. She wouldn't take no for an answer and was a bold woman in Christ. He knew on their first date, this vivacious cheerleader, was his one and only. She was equally smitten with the newly graduated attractive, ambitious, ROTC Captain.

Carol was always stepping out and trying new things. Jim, though, was much more focused. During Operation Desert Storm his helicopter got caught in a Simoon (dust storm), and went down. Luckily, Jim survived but his co-pilot did not. As a result, injuries sent him back home to the good old United States of America. After he finished his commitment to the Air Force, Jim returned to teach at his alma mater in Denver, Colorado. By then, Carol produced their firstborn, a son named Greg...

While Jim was overseas Carol became involved with a genuine group of Christians and began to seriously read the Bible and dedicated her life to Jesus Christ.

Greg was born a premature child and although he was small, Carol concentrated a lot of her prayer life in helping him to grow. He was intelligent. So much so, that Carol made sure that he was constantly being challenged to do his best. He was always at the top of his class. They were proud of their son, even in death as he drowned to save his buddy.

***

His desk phone jangled, alerting Jim for his next appointment of the day. At the same time Carol just finished her morning Bible study when a message arrived that her exercise class would be cancelled. She decided to go on a brisk spring walk through the woods since she and the girls were at their cabin. The air was refreshing as she slipped a soft red crew neck sweater over her head and began walking.

She closed her eyes, inhaled deeply and started to think. She loved it up here in the mountains. Maybe she would see some wildlife if she could be quiet enough. Two squirrels scampered by and something upset some scrub jays ahead.

Although she felt a deep peace, yet there was a still a slight nagging in her soul, like unfinished business. Her family was all prayed for and whatever else that she could think of. *What was it?* Carol wondered how her elderly parents were. She would have to speak with Jim about helping them out more as soon as he left office.

Jim...she began to fondly remember their first meeting. *Was he a catch or what?* Lots of girls on campus were after him.

He was very tall and after they became an item, their friends used to call them "Mutt and Jeff." The first thing he told her was that he wanted to be President when he grew up and she responded that she wanted to the President's wife when she grew up! She did not know what being married to a politician would involve. She always felt very inadequate and ill prepared for her duties as the Vice-President's wife. She bravely took on ever increasing responsibilities which caused her to be on her knees daily for God's help and grace. She graduated from college as a teacher and enjoyed a real gift to see where people needed help. Jim relied heavily on her wit and wisdom.

Snowflakes began to tickle Carol's nose as she jogged down the back path toward their cabin. Her girls ran ahead of her, laughing and playing in the crisp air. Carol laughed with them as they praised the Lord together. The weather was so hot yesterday and even this morning, Montana reported one hundred plus degree weather at sunrise.

Carol's cell phone alerted her that Jim's office was calling. The secretary couldn't find him. She left him laying down for a rest before his midmorning appointment. Did Carol know where he might be?

Carol and the girls gasped as they heard the words, "Come up!" It was a loving command and as they obeyed, reaching their arms towards the morning sun, there was Jim and their beloved Savior along with the rest of their families.

"Oh My God, you've kept your promise to save our entire household! You came back, Jesus! Thank you! I love you!" Everyone moving upward was full of worship and praise.

Chapter 30

Dana Jones yawned and stretched as much as the leg room would allow. *Amazing*, she thought to herself, *how could such an expensive seat on a jumbo jet be so darned small?* She flew into San Francisco, California from Hawaii. She sat in first class. Although night flights were more expensive because of the intense day storms and heat, she needed to be in New York City by midnight Eastern Standard Time. It was three o'clock a.m. Pacific Time. She and her fellow players accepted an hour layover and they were given no choice but to travel tonight.

Dana was part of a play called, "The Passion." The troupe of players had a window of opportunity to be able to do a two night stint in New York City. Her character, Mary Magdalene, fit her perfectly with her green eyes and long auburn hair.

Christianity was at an all time low and they were excited about their ministry. Each player believed that they had been brought together to share their love of Jesus Christ and this was their purpose on earth to spread the gospel. They always prayed together before the play and encouraged the audience to participate throughout and afterwards, an alter call was given.

"Come on guys," one of the actors suggested to his fellow players. "Let's get off and move around. We've got an hour before our next flight and I'm starved. Water for five hours is not what I want." Regulations became so strict that even crew members could not eat. Nor were the passengers allowed to carry snacks on board.

The little band of Christian players opted for a quick submarine sandwich and sat in a solarium in the middle of the airport. The finer restaurants were crowded and they would not have enough time to get back to the waiting plane.

Dana settled back into her seat which reclined somewhat. The extra expense for such a long direct flight was worth it. Second class seats were even smaller and didn't move.

She was cold and after covering herself with an air travel blanket, fell fast asleep. The last thing she remembered as she rolled over to her side was the morning star in a clear eastern sky over Reno, Nevada.

Purring through the early morning with a strong tail wind, the crew and passengers were encouraged that their estimated time of arrival would be much sooner than expected. Everyone settled into quiet.

Suddenly the plane lurched forward. It was such a hard jolt that some whose seatbelts were unfastened hit the floor! Seatbelt lights switched on and the captain apologized saying that they had encountered an unexpected electrical storm. Before he could finish his statement, there was another flash and strike. Most people were used to the rough weather but when the curtains between the crew and passengers were drawn back, chaos ensued. Standing there in the front of the cabin was a huge man with his hands outstretched. All over the plane people began to bow. Believers and non-believers began to worship the pure light coming from the man. The captain came forward; his face white, and fell to his knees. "My Lord," he responded, as Jesus called his brothers and sisters to Him.

Dana and several passengers, including their captain were moving upward above the plane as it took a slight dip and began a terrifying descent! There were people all around Dana and her friends.

Although she was moving upwards, she could see somehow supernaturally as she watched the plane fall to the ground. She observed other humans all over the world below. They were losing control of their vehicles on Interstate 80 and in cities and towns. A train ran off the tracks and other aircraft were falling from the sky, above and below them. Everyone seemed to understand or know that this was truly Jesus. Dana noticed that many people were floating upwards as they praised and worshipped the one true God. She felt light and airy as tears filled her eyes. She realized what was happening. She wondered about other people and felt compassion for the remaining souls that she sensed would not be going with her. She remembered reading about these things in the Bible. Then she became full of peace and joy as she joined a chorus of singing in a sky filled with saints and angels.

Chapter 31

    Although Sam possessed plenty of proof as to his innocence, circumstances once imprisoned, were hard to change. He had been set up by his partner in a world trade business. His partner embezzled from their company and took off leaving Sam to suffer the consequences. Court systems were totally corrupt. If a prisoner had any money to be gotten, it was certain that everyone knew. A prison with corrupt judges, lawyers, and prison chaplains was all that was left of a once flourishing Democracy in the United States. Sam's chances of ever getting out of prison were very slim. He was out of money and with no family left to extort money out of, the system would finally leave him alone.

    He bucked too much when he was younger and like many others over thirty years of age; the system believed the prisoners were too old to be rehabilitated. Because it was too expensive to keep them incarcerated, many prisoners just disappeared after the age of forty.

    Sam found Jesus to be real in his life and he began to read the Bible and pray while he was in prison. Falsely accused as a young man, he did his best to serve his sentence after all his options for help failed. Sam was full of tattoos and although he looked tough, he was one of the most loved men in the federal prison system. He got the tattoos when he was first incarcerated. He believed that they would help discourage fellow prisoners that would otherwise bother him. There were more times than Sam could count that he was supernaturally protected in a bad prison system. The man had never been married and after some time all of his relatives died. He was alone now and wondered if there was any purpose left in his life. He knew his life had been spared several times. He seemed to have a calming effect on those around him and was able to talk fellow prisoners into different ways of thinking.

Because of Sam's change in behavior, he eventually gained more privileges than most. He could get a semi-monthly shower, a weekly outdoor walk in the compound, and a very small fine print New Testament to read. He began to read and pray daily. He was luckier than most because he was literate unlike many of his fellow prisoners. Some of the guards relied on him for his ability to communicate, in a mixture of broken Mexican and Spanish which was a second language in the United States. Even good English was hard for some groups to understand. The vocabulary in both languages was poor. Sam had a unique comical way of speaking that everyone seemed to understand and enjoy. Once a tall good looking man of Spanish descent, he still enjoyed a full head of black hair. He possessed excellent skills at imitating anyone he came in contact with and often times could get people to laugh. He was serious though in quiet times and sincerely believed that Jesus Christ would return.

He thought to himself how like his life was compared to George Orwell's book, *1984*. The government became Big Brother. Control over his life felt overwhelming. There he was in his small cell with a bed, toilet, and big screen television. He could pull in only one channel with a program that constantly barked out orders. Every hour a negative world news report would come on with three minutes of weather reports thrown in. *What did he care when he could only go out for short periods of time?* He thought dismally.

One morning, much to Sam's surprise, he found himself on top of the prison tower. A golden sun was just rising. He inhaled a deep breath of fresh air and smiled as he lifted his hands upwards in praise. All of a sudden a shout rang out and reverberated across the brilliant sky. "Come up!" the voice commanded. Sam started shaking realizing that he must have escaped and he was in a lot of trouble. The light grew more intense and he saw a man on a white horse and the light grew brighter. Then there were angels and singing!

"Come Sam, take my hand, and don't be afraid," Sam gasped and sank to his knees, overwhelmed. "Oh! My God! My Lord! You returned!"

As Sam began to move upwards, he looked down and he was pleased to see others, some whom he prayed with to receive Christ as their personal Savior. Some also, who didn't understand what fellowship meant. There was a judge as well from years ago. He was a man who tried to help Sam in the end; he slipped a note to Sam asking for prayer support in a sick broken system.

Chapter 32

Frank Collins was a slightly built nerdy-type person. By the time he graduated from college, he had a receding hairline. Although he was middle aged, his knowledge of the computer world put him into a secure high security position with the One World Government under the United States. He was able to avoid the military by opting for a special selection process in which he worked between special agencies like the FBI and CIA, including the OWG. After the 9/11 bombing of the two Trade Towers in New York City, he was in charge of getting the World States Security forces united. Frank was at the top of his field when he met David.

Unassuming Frank had been married for a brief time. He didn't have any children and was an only child himself. His parents died long ago. Frank's father and mother were well educated. Well traveled throughout the world, they provided an excellent upbringing, including all the latest computers and Play Stations a little boy could want. Being religious people, they exposed him to all types of faiths, but the young person had little interest in anything other than computers and mother boards. Frank never figured out why his bored wife left him for an exciting military officer who would take her to wonderful new places around the globe.

Frank was so busy preparing for a one world system that he hardly noticed when she tearfully left. He preferred an occasional dinner date with a fine red wine and an attractive female who expected nothing from him, but the money he spent so freely. He lived well and life was simple with no strings attached.

One of Frank's vices included spending hours on the internet. He graduated at the top of his college class. However, he, like many of his peers did not acquire a rounded education. He could talk for hours to fellow computer geeks, but realized he was surrounded by those with alternate lifestyles. He didn't really care but he liked to carry on an intelligent conversation from time to time. He was amused that most professionals didn't understand his job either. They would have been very surprised. Their careers kept them way too busy trying to get to the top of their fields.

The beginning of the century found computer systems taking a new leap in progress. New technology put the new world system in place.

As a director and overseer of implementation and formatting worldwide computers to be compatible, Frank was able to put engineers and technicians in their place to keep things running smoothly.

Frank's time was becoming freer and he could get on the super-highway more often for recreation. He never enjoyed outdoor activities. One of the people on his staff challenged him concerning some ancient manuscripts. He told Frank that he could probably find the answers he was looking for in biblical history. It was in one of those old history books that he ran head on into a man named Jesus Christ of Nazareth. For the first time in his life, Frank began to develop an interest in something other than computers.

Although Frank was a world traveler, he was based in Chicago, Ill, USA. He spent a lot of time traveling back and forth between Washington D.C. and Luxemburg, Belgium, where the OWG money system was headquartered. Frank and his co-worker David often traveled together. They were working on implementing a cashless society.

Frank was amazed at some of the parallels and warnings in the Bible that he discovered. There was also a lot of information in many of the prophetic and science fiction books written near the end of the twentieth century. He began to develop a thirst for knowledge about this man, Jesus Christ. He became insatiable. The more he learned, the more he wanted to know. He hadn't given God a thought his entire life, let alone God's son, Jesus. Could it be possible that there was a God? He began spending more time on the internet and talking out loud to himself. Often, in front of people, he would sound crazy and he was gaining the reputation of being rather eccentric. Of course, in the twenty-first century, anyone over thirty was rather old and odd. Years ago people would accuse one another of having a "senior moment" if they were forgetful.

As time went forward, Frank began to seek Jesus. He broke down late one evening and challenged God; if He was "really around" then Frank wanted to know more about Him.

Frank began to experience things and people that he never noticed before. His world expanded as he studied Christian and Jewish religions.

Most Jews returned to their homeland of Israel (which after seven years of peace, was quite messed up). The few Christians that Frank was familiar with were pretty quiet. There was a lot of persecution around the world the past ten years and Christians were considered an enemy everywhere. Since they were against the OWG and its policies, Christians claimed one true God and were not accepting that many different cultures have their own Gods.

This Christian religion was not considered tolerant of other people and their beliefs. Therefore, they were not accepted either.

For some reason Frank began to run into more and more of these people. He began to understand and embrace their viewpoints. One of the things he noticed was that most of society was losing a lot of personal freedom in lieu of the OWG.

David was a top notch news reporter on a worldwide newscast station. Frank was impressed with David's persuasive skills. This reporter explained away many doubts and questionable acts that the United States government was doing, all in the name of World Peace. While Frank was constantly revising computer systems, David was convincing countries to accept the latest technology. Frank was impressed with how David and "the team" handled implementing the bar code.

A bright sun came streaming through Frank's window as his alarm sounded. He yawned, stretched, and rose from his desk chair, headed for the bathroom, muttering to himself that because he forgot to pull the shades on the window, the sun caused a glare on his computer screen. Before he realized it, he had been surfing all night. He was just about to try a new video game when the morning rays hit the screen.

Warm smells of timed French roast coffee floated through the shower curtain as Frank turned off the water and stepped out, pleased that he remembered to set the coffee maker to brew early. *Hmmm…he thought to himself. I wonder where David is.* No one had heard from him in a few months. The time frame for the bar-code mark on people was coming up soon and Frank needed to discuss some minor details with David. Frank needed to do some final tweaking in the world system program. Things were tied all together and running smoothly around the world. The powers to be decided that it would be a good idea to let things run this way for awhile so the world could get used to the idea. This also gave the OWG a chance to point out all the good things about the implementation.

Now, time to open the subject of a world-wide mark. David had done a good job thus far but where was he? No one seemed to know except that he was sent to Israel. Frank and the rest of the team were short of the facts and Frank became annoyed. He and David always shared and worked together. It was tough about what happened to David's wife. Frank figured maybe David was resting. He rubbed his chin in thought and looked at his face in the mirror, deep in thought. *But why Israel? What a dumb place for rest and recreation. There were hundreds of more desirable government places for the employees to go to enjoy a quick vacation.* Only one person that Frank thought he could trust to ask was the Vice-President. The man and his family could not be reached though.

The Vice-President left a message not long after he retired that he didn't want to be disturbed for a couple of months. Most people did not know that the Vice-President was still working. He told everyone he retired and was wrapping things up at the office. His boss, wanted him to do things in this manner because of the Vice-President's health. Frank liked the family. They were always kind to him. Once or twice Frank detected there was something very different. He knew the Vice-President was experiencing some heart trouble so maybe that accounted for some of his odd behavior.

The Vice-President had been quite argumentative in his early years. He never seemed to be one hundred percent committed to the President and world policy. Frank noticed the past few years that the man was becoming more reserved. People around D.C. shared rumors that the Vice-President and his wife belonged to a group of fanatical Christians out in the Colorado area. "Oh well," the slight man mused out loud. "It doesn't matter. People are doing weird things all over the world. If that's the case then they will be shut down soon enough."

Shut down, that was the next step after people accepted the

bar-code. There were always little Christian groups popping up around the world. Most of them were irritants and rag tag groups. A lot of them went underground but without the mark, it was going to be very hard to buy and sell items of all sorts.

They wouldn't be able to do any type of banking that was for sure. The uprisings were quickly shut up and if there was a newsworthy story, it would be maximized to the advantage of the OWG. Sometimes, events escalated and to maintain control, protestors would be shot for the sake of the majority. Frank thought governments appeared to be a little too rough. For years, he kept focused on his job and was quiet. With time on his hands though, he began to think about other people more often.

***

Frank came into his condominium after a tough, hard day of work. "At last this part of the bar code is finished." He spoke out loud to the empty room. Over-tired, he fell into bed without dinner or even undressing. Most of time Frank never dreamed except was when he was sick or had actually gotten some exercise. Tonight was an exception. He tossed fitfully from one side of his king sized bed to another. He saw strange animals and heard screaming that raised hair on the nape of his neck. Several times he got up to go to the bathroom. Around midnight he awoke to a laugh that was unmistakable. He heard it once, as a child and remembered the terror he relived one snowy Halloween night. He ran to his parents arms convinced there was a witch that chased after him. Frank opened his eyes to find himself in the spirit world. There were forms around the room taunting him and arguing about who he belonged to. "He's mine," cackled the witch. "No." Another form hissed.

A man in white appeared. "Leave him alone!" The commanding voice came forth from this person. "He belongs to me!"

***

Frank was so frightened; he ran into the bathroom and blew chunks. He came back to his bed shaking with fear. He shivered as he made his way to turn the thermostat higher on the heater and after adding a blanket to the bed, he crawled underneath. Frank covered his head. The next morning the phone woke him. "Frank, this is the Vice-President. Don't talk, just listen. You experienced a rough night huh?"

"Well, yeah, but how did you know?" Frank said.

"I just know. God has put you on my heart to pray for. You need to find David. You also need to understand Jesus Christ is your personal Savior. Don't accept the bar-code on your body Frank. It's too dangerous!" The Vice-President told him about a little known government document to get a hold of to read. He also told him to find a Bible and read it.

"You are one of them." Frank gasped. "But why are you calling me?"

"Because God told me to and it's that simple. I have to go, there is a good possibility I'm being taped," and with that the man hung up.

Frank fell back into a deep sleep and woke up at noon. He tried to get rid of the previous night. He took a cup of hot coffee to his study and fired up his computer. He found where David was approximately and put in a request to take some files with him that they could only work on together. He convinced his supervisor that the trip would be worthwhile and he wouldn't take much down time.

Soon a reply came back that he could go in a couple of weeks. One of his technicians couldn't be found and one quit, so some programs in their work needed adjustment. He was ordered to get bar-coded before he left so he was able to get around on the world travel system. In addition to those orders, he was to remind David that he still needed to get his identification mark as well. Frank was careful not to ask about details. He knew how to break into higher security systems that were beyond his classifications, but he never allowed anyone to know what he had access to. Circumstances caused Frank to become suspicious of everyone. He always felt confident in his position as long as he was briefed on everyone involved. There were too many unanswered questions in his life right now.

Soon he found the documents he was looking for concerning specifics on what to do with people who would not accept the mark. Frank became more dismayed as he read on. Sure, he had seen persecution here and there. They were small unorganized uprisings that needed to be quieted down, but this was an actual shut down. People would be notified by e-mail to begin the process. Those who did not have an e-mail address were sent a certified letter. Within ten days of receiving their notices, they were to report to the nearest social security office. Or, in some rural areas, that would be the nearest Post Office. At their specified location they would be processed into the system. They were asked to already have made a choice as to whether they preferred their "special" identification mark: to be implemented on their hands or foreheads. The skin must be cleaned for preparation and they must wear white clothing for computer scanners. There were serious consequences if these orders were not adhered to. Anything from fines, tortures, even threat of imprisonment or death as an example to others that they must comply was included in the sent orders.

A cashless society would insure peace and most people were willing to obey. The majority were all too eager to have more security and world peace even if it meant giving up more freedoms. No one in this generation enjoyed the freedoms their grandparents once experienced as children. Changes were so subtle that the public was lulled into a false sense of reality and security. Important documents Frank guarded were clearly separating riff-raff from the rest of the world. News Media played a huge part by constantly bombarding world population with daily doses of brain washing news. Frank didn't know what to do with the frightening information he obtained. He began saying the wrong things to the wrong people. Twice his superior called him to warn him, perhaps he needed a rest?

Frank managed to get his appointment for his mark pushed ahead a number of times but he was short on time. He knew he could offer a couple of excuses, one being the horrible new strain of flu going around. He missed his annual inoculation which was a combination this year of several diseases that returned since the beginning of the twentieth century. His job took him to Brussels and so he had to try to re-schedule. He was fined heavily for that mistake. As a result, he could buy some time with the excuse of illness. He also managed to have car troubles and confusion on his schedule. He kept remembering the warning he received last month in the middle of the night.

One day in the break room at work, a co-worker waited around until there was only Frank and himself. "Excuse me Frank?"

"Yes," Frank turned round. "What do you want?" He did not recognize this person.

Dark and muscular, a strange man pulled a small pocket Bible from his jacket and shoved it into Frank's hands. "This is for you Frank. God told me to give it to you. Read the Book of John and..." A group of co-workers came around the corner and entered the room interrupting the man.

Frank began reading as soon as he got home. He was insatiable again and before he realized how late it was, the morning sun began to rise.

"I can't go over today and get my mark." Frank told his superior. "I have to get on the plane in the morning for Israel." His boss told him that he needed to be there for David and Frank to get coded because they should have been the first and here it was almost a month later. His job was on the line if they didn't get this done by the end of the week. Frank shivered to himself, not only had he seen what was happening to those who refused the mark but people who sported it were definitely taking a superior attitude over those who weren't displaying it. Of course, one could choose not to have a distinguishing mark. It could be invisible on the forehead or hand but the media was making people accept it as a "special" item of fashion. Most people were proud to bear it, they belonged to the OWG. Humanistic and natural, it was a status symbol. It was cool to belong to a group; the majority couldn't understand what all the emotion was about. Traveling abroad was easier. Not only money, but passports were unnecessary. There were all sorts of incentives offered, free flying miles and free liquor with free meals. Many didn't know the repercussions, but Frank did. All loss of medical help included prescription drugs. No loans for homes. No one could buy or sell anything. Those who refused were gathered in groups for interrogation, then individual counseling and eventually terminated for the good of the world.

    Most of these remnants went underground and tried to help care for one another. Sharing whatever excesses they could find. This became a terrifying world to live in if one had some insight into the whole picture.

    Frank was on OWG payroll so he could still move about with his OWG card as long as he watched what he was using it for. Anything to do with the trip would be safe for awhile.

    His loud alarm clock clanged announcing the day's upcoming schedule and Frank was so sleepy he could hardly move. He rolled out of bed and stumbled to the bathroom for some allergy pills and water. The late night and lack of sleep didn't help matters. He stuffed the small Bible into his inner coat pocket as he dressed for the trip. Security wasn't as difficult for him so he was able to carry the Bible in his pocket.

"Good morning Sir!" A tall vivacious hostess met him at the first class checkpoint and directed him to his assigned aircraft where she turned his seat outward for him to sit in. Her bright OWG multicolored uniform reminded him of a parrot. He was still drowsy so accepted her offer of coffee. A seasoned traveler, he elected to forego breakfast and as he clutched a colorful pillow and matching blanket, he fell asleep. The time went so fast, that before he knew it, she was shaking his shoulders and waking him for lunch. As soon as he was full, he pulled out his Bible and began reading. He was amazed that there were so many warnings and prophetic happenings that he witnessed himself the last thirty years. He remembered his grandparents telling him about Jesus and salvation but he was very young and his parents would tell him all religions have the same God and He was whoever one wanted Him to be. God had many names, according to the majority of people. Most of his peers believed the same, including all of his educators. This had been ingrained from pre-school on throughout his formal education. No one ever shared that he could have a personal friendship with the man Jesus Christ. Or for that matter, that this was absolute truth. Frank read for himself that Jesus was the only way, the truth, and the life. The more he read, the more he understood why he shouldn't be marked. He also realized many God-fearing people were more afraid of man and began to go underground, not sharing the good news and salvation promises. They were well meaning but after all, human. The OWG accomplished a good job in causing people to be full of fear.

***

Frank thought he was dreaming when he heard someone in

a loving voice commanding him to come.

Bright light spilled throughout the cabin. Although, it was nighttime and they were flying over the water, the light flashed. It appeared to be coming from the right wing near Frank's window. The plane was quiet inside and no one seemed to notice anything unusual. Frank spoke to the voice in his dream. "I can't come through the window; it's too small for me. Who are you? What do you want?" He suddenly saw himself out on the wing with the light swirling around him.

"Sleep my son," the voice again commanded.

"Lord, is that you?" Frank whispered.

"I am that I am," was the reply he heard.

Speechless, Frank looked below him to see the entire plane take a steep left bank and dive into the ocean far below.

Days later, Frank found himself wet and cold. His eyes burned from salt water and he was having difficulty focusing. He assumed that it was day time, maybe early in the morning because it seemed to him that there was some light outside. Judging by the temperature it must be daybreak. He remembered little of what took place but realized that he was in a lot of trouble.

He fell asleep again, very troubled about what he was recalling. Dirty and confused he woke to voices and people prodding him. He hoped they spoke English because all he could hear was an accent that sounded rather far Eastern.

At last he was awake enough to speak. "Help me please. Does anyone speak English? Where am I?" He still could not see but he smelled the ocean nearby and a hint of food, enough that he felt his stomach growl. He sat up and spit gritty sand out of his mouth. His clothes were wet and he heard a little girl answer. Frank shook his head as if to clear it and hoped that his ears and eyes weren't playing tricks on him. His eyes stung worse than earlier and he tried to wipe them with the back of his hand.

"I speak English Sir. You are in the country of Israel. My

mother and father are here with two of my brothers. My brothers speak some English too but they are younger so don't understand everything you are saying. Are you hurt?"

"No, I think I'm okay but I can't see very well," Frank widened his eyes.

"My parents say to me, for you to come home with us. They will help you. Do you have a name?"

For a fleeting moment, Frank felt cautious so he told them his first name. He hoped that maybe he could trust someone. He wasn't going to let them know how badly his eyes were hurting. He could see light but couldn't make out images. Grateful, he accepted the two little boy's hands on either side of him.

Soon they arrived in a small village of sorts and Frank was led into a dark shelter. He was given something like warm bouillon or tea. It refreshed him at once and soon he and the little girl began a more intense conversation. She was eager to help and her words bounced between Frank, her family and herself.

He soon learned that he was indeed in Israel and he would be well cared for. He found out that his plane went down with the news that there were no survivors. As far as this village knew, there were no other people found. Frank was relieved to hear that he purchased more time in avoiding the mark. He couldn't see if anyone displayed a distinguishing mark so as his confidence grew, he asked if they had a trade mark on their bodies. They told him none of the village people were accepting it. They were what were called a group of completed Jews. Frank didn't understand the meaning so he asked for a definition. The little girl struggled but finally got him to understand who they were. Most of the village was Jewish and a lot of them had given their lives to Jesus Christ, rejecting the mark according to what the Bible warned them about. The Book instructed believers not to accept a mark and not to be afraid because Jesus would be returning. They would help and care for one another until Jesus returned for his people. Frank told them that he was on his way to Jerusalem to find David Roberts. He told them who David was without saying too much; he explained who he was as well. They understood enough and said they would send word out but he would have to understand that extra caution was necessary to protect each other. The family wanted to know why he hadn't accepted the mark if he really was who he said. Frank explained that he wasn't ready and unsure about what was happening. They accepted his excuse and shared that they would pray for him.

Two days later, the children came running home to let everyone know that they heard of this fellow David. He was indeed in Jerusalem. Local people told him that he and his little band were living in the evil caves outside of town near the cemetery and he was a madman! He wore sackcloth with some other nut-case, was disheveled and walked the streets of the Great City crying "Repent! Repent!" all day long. The believers in the area declared he was one of the two prophets described in the Book of Revelations.

To non-believers they were annoying beyond words. Frank couldn't see to read so he asked the young girl to read Revelation to him. He was scared at how much things began to fit his old co-worker. Frank asked the group of villagers if they could get him to David. He was afraid to say much to anyone for fear of hurting his new little family. Each one hugged him goodbye and the little girl explained that they were all praying for him and wished him God-speed. Two village elders walked with him, sensing his lack of sight, they kept bringing him back onto the right path. One spoke English very well and the other was a happy amiable person so before he knew it, Frank was in Jerusalem. All three men spent the night in a fellow Christian's home.

The next morning they went out and before Frank realized what happened, there was a lot of confusion in the streets and Frank was disconnected from his new friends. He was afraid to call out so he circled, trying to be as inconspicuous as possible. He heard shots ringing out in the streets and people shouting as they ran away for shelter. He found himself lost and wandering the streets of Jerusalem. He did not know how many days or weeks he was alone. He began to feel uncomfortable and his whole body ached and itched. He befriended a stray dog with a bit of fish. He proved to be helpful in finding food and water for both of them.

Then…he heard an old familiar voice. "Leave that man alone!" Bullets flew around him and cries of victory echoed as he heard bodies thudding down in the dusty street. His eyes gave out in a cloud of gunfire and dirty grit.

"David! David! Is that you?" he shouted.

Chapter 33

Down shifting the grinding gears, medium built Kevin Speck concentrated on getting to the top of Grapevine Hill on Interstate 5 to Los Angeles, California. The big semi-truck was due for an over-haul when he returned to the main office in Denver, Colorado. It was dark but he knew as soon as he got to the top, it would be bright. Light pollution was bad in this area. People could no longer enjoy the stars. There were vehicles trailing down on the opposite side of the freeway. They reminded him of a stream of moving red fire ants. He shook his full head of neatly trimmed white hair in amazement. There was a lot of traffic because it was Spring Break. Decades back, it would have been Good Friday, a day in history that Kevin's Savior had been crucified over two thousand years ago.

At the top of the hill, the truck lurched and Kevin quickly found a place to pull over for the rest of the night. He planned to dump his load off early, as soon as the store opened. Then he could pull into Denver sometime on Sunday. He needed to pick up a driver trainee in Reno, Nevada so he would be able to get his rest while he set a pace for the trainee east on Interstate 80 to Salt Lake City, Utah. That wouldn't be too difficult for the new driver. He finished school so all was required was to make sure he earned his hours and mileage experience for a license to become an independent driver.

Kevin climbed up into his bunk and read for a few minutes in his Bible and then turned out the reading light. He was uncomfortable and woke several times. He thought of his wife, Cheryl, who died ten years earlier in her late forties. Kevin still cried for her, having a hard time accepting that modern science still couldn't find more help for female cancer problems. In his sixties now, Kevin was getting tired and missed her every day. He had been a career officer in the Air Force but soon after retirement, Cheryl became ill. She suffered a long time and when the tall slender woman passed away, Kevin decided to make some changes in his life. Kevin and Cheryl loved to travel, so Kevin continued in this way, traveling back and forth across the country. He was always meeting new people. He never lacked for friends.

***

"Good morning Joe." Kevin greeted the store manager in Riverside, California. He received a reply in the form of a big handshake.

"Hey! How is it going? I've got two kids here who wanted to work this weekend so unloading will only take a few minutes," the big burly man grinned, pleased with himself.

Within a half hour Kevin was fueling up and on his way again. He decided to head up a newly constructed freeway through Nevada since the weather was pleasant. The desert was brilliant and beautiful in the springtime since it was getting more rain-fall there. Most of the traffic this weekend would be up and down the coast. There were a lot of small retirement towns cropping up. It appeared as if older people were being forced to move in this direction. Housing and medicine proved to be cheaper. Climate warm, it was rather attractive to the older generation with arthritis. They would sell out and look around down here in the winter, like it, and move in. Many though became disappointed in the summer. Summers were unbearable and air conditioning was expensive. Humidity was at an all time high because of all the water and man-made rice paddies. Water was being brought down from other states, depleting the natural supply up in the Sierra and Rocky Mountains. Climates were just the opposite of what they once were around the world. At least as far back since Kevin was a boy and could remember. Ice caps were melting at an alarming rate and heavy snows would fall where snow was unheard of. It was not only because of seasonal weather changes but because of manipulation of ancient water systems. This was not natural as many leaders with scare tactics suggested. Global Weather Warnings brought about fear and guilt. People didn't realize that many things around the earth were natural disasters. Nightly news brought it closer to home and instead of hearing of one at a time, the news could report several global storms at one time.

***

With an empty truck, Kevin made it to Reno with time to spare so he met his trainee, cleaned up, and they enjoyed a good dinner together. The two drivers decided to leave about six in the morning.

Kevin was worried when he got his new guy in place. Tony was a small Italian man who appeared to be unsure of his driving skills. Kevin breathed a sigh of relief when he saw that the man could reach all of the equipment necessary to drive the big rig. Tony clearly wanted to do a good job and please him. Kevin, being thirty years his senior realized what he needed to do to help this younger person.

He began to learn about him. Tony wasn't married and his family lived back east. He had a formal education but didn't like working with computers and he didn't make it through a doctor's program. He decided to just take time off and run around the country for awhile. As time went on, Tony shared that he was interested in all types of religions and beliefs. He started reading the Bible; much to the dismay of his family and peers. That gave Kevin an opportunity to share his faith in Jesus and the plan of salvation with Tony. Tony was interested and asked many questions, eventually leading to some serious prayer time and Tony accepting Jesus Christ as his personal Savior.

Before they realized it, they were near Salt Lake City. Kevin asked Tony if he was an early driver or if he preferred night driving. Kevin was happy to find out that Tony was a night driver. "Tell you what Tony; you've done a good job all day. We'll stop on the other side of the city and rest. I'll drive through the heavy construction on the east side. You did great getting out of Reno, but this is a real tough place to navigate. There are one way dirt exits all over. I'm hungry and this old truck needs to rest as much as I do. Let's plan to leave about four in the morning. How does that sound?" Tony was exhausted and he was in total agreement with the plan.

For dinner they inhaled a hearty steak with a country western band playing on a stage. When the waitress brought the tab, Kevin pulled out the company credit card.

"Since no one takes cash any longer, when do I get one of those?" Tony joked.

"When you get your hours completed and if the company hires you," grinned Kevin. "Now don't look so afraid; you're doing fine."

Tony questioned him. "Well, can you answer me as a Christian? There is something I don't understand and I hope you can help me. I found in my reading in the Bible about a mark. That people can't buy or sell without it. First I thought this was all too silly but…the last few months our government seems to be pressuring the people that way with no options. Then I saw on the news the other night that the OWG is pushing this as well. I spoke with a couple of old college buddies and they laughed at me and asked where I'd been all six years of college?" Tony rolled his eyes. "My dad told me to get my head out of the sand and get a life. I tell you Kevin, I've been interested in helping people and animals when they are sick. I gave up the attempt because I don't believe in euthanasia which is so prevalent today. Kevin, I've seen miracles, if that is what you can still call them! People and animals can sometimes get better and no one is able to give me a clear answer as to why," Tony pleaded for understanding.

Kevin was amazed at the sweet nature of his new friend. The compassion he saw reminded him of his precious Cheryl and her faith in Christ. "You know Tony; it is so interesting that you asked me about this mark. I am keenly aware of what it is about. Cheryl and I prayed together and discussed at great lengths as to what we would do should we have to make a decision in our lifetime. Thank goodness, Cheryl doesn't have to now. I, on the other hand have been notified by mail that I have to have a mark by my sixty-fifth birthday. I may either have it on my hand or my forehead. It can be visible or invisible. I have no alternatives. I will lose my trucking license and not be able to use this on board computer to receive my paychecks or take care of personal business, like paying my bills. I will lose the privilege of doctors and medications. I also know of several people and friends who have refused to get this done. The consequences are pretty scary. A couple of people have died for no apparent reasons as well. I can't tell you what to do. All I know is that it is real and I have already decided not to accept the mark myself. A good book to read, if you can even find it, is George Orwell's *1984*. Although it is fiction, there is a lot about losing our freedoms to a Big Brother System or

One World Government. Many people dismissed it as pure fiction. Some felt it was very poor writing. But, to others it became frightening as they watched the world progress around them."

"Thank you for being so friendly and sharing with me Kevin," Tony said. The two men each got a motel room.

Tony woke up with a peace that he never experienced before. He began praising his new found Lord. It seemed so pleasant to him to give control of his life to someone else. Someone he could trust who was bigger and all-knowing. Tony felt comfort in accepting his new freedom. He prayed and asked for help in not accepting a mark of any type on his body. He asked for extra faith and trust to live without it. He asked for grace to walk in his new faith, although he didn't understand grace. He told God that he wanted to learn as much as he could. Much to Tony's surprise, he got a response. The voice was audible, so commanding, yet loving and clear, there was no doubt as to whom it belonged.

"I have watched you Tony, from your conception. I have waited for you to come and talk with me. I love you individually because you love and accept my Son. Don't worry about the future. I will show you what to do. Jesus is coming back. Look for Him in the Eastern sky."

They finished up a good breakfast and firing up the truck, started the last leg of their run. To their dismay, the news ahead was not good. A huge snow storm hit the mountains just east of the city. The weather pattern was abnormal and the weather forecasters missed their forecasts the majority of the time. There were reports of avalanches all over the freeway and many accidents ahead. Kevin suggested that he continue beyond the construction and on into the storm. He told Tony not to worry about his accumulating hours because he could go on with him on the next assigned run. Tony gratefully accepted the idea.

Hours went by and conditions became worse with each

mile. Kevin couldn't remember a worse storm. He was surprised that the Interstate was being kept open. There were horrible accidents all around where vehicles slid off the freeway.

Both men noticed at the same time, a bright light ahead. They blinked as all of a sudden they were standing on top of their cab outside as it careened out of control down into a valley. They were lifted up and continued upwards. The higher they went, the more they saw. There was wreckage as far as they could see from east to west. The men saw a ball of light coming from the east and walking out of it was Jesus telling everyone watching and listening to come to Him. Many people were in the air singing and embracing each other as they obeyed. Kevin and Tony eagerly joined the believers and singing angels.

Chapter 34

Year 1

The caves were full of candle light; John and David's eyes were still trying to focus as they stepped out into the bright morning sun. They started their preaching by trying to explain the previous weekend events. John's preaching was on fire with warnings of repentance. David shared about the mark of the beast and OWG and how computers were involved.

Every evening, they returned to John's room to pray and re-group. By the end of the week, they were turned out of their room. John had no money left so David suggested they take his remaining funds and give them to the prayer group in the caves. They would be staying there from now on. Jennifer was a good manager of money and she could get whatever provisions the group needed.

"I have to call the Vice-President of the United States." David was urgent as he tried to get loose ends in his mind resolved. Much to his relief, the whole family seemed to be gone.

As the year rolled on, the summer became hotter. The world moved into its third year of drought and water seemed scarce. Fires were out of control. There wasn't enough water to put out raging forest fires in North American and land, people, and animals were becoming parched.

Fear was at epidemic proportions and people were more afraid of their neighbors than of terrorists. Especially annoying were two men running around the streets of Jerusalem. They were like mosquitoes and locusts in their unending quest. People were bothered by their accusations, saying all this devastation was their own faults and to repent as if they brought this upon themselves. They were becoming touchy about anything having to do with Christianity. They were hoping things would settle down when the majority of this cult was gone. It took about six months for the world to realize that there were a lot less so called Christians running around. They were saying good riddance to those goody-two shoes, now they could begin to enjoy their sins and unbelief. Citizens of the world became more materialistic and lovers of selves. If it felt good then it must be okay. As long as you don't hurt anyone else, it is fine to act as you please the people believed. Humanity was so self-absorbed, that they were not even aware how they individually affected people around them. John remembered the scriptures being turned around where people would become confused between right from wrong in their beliefs, morals, and values. People began to believe all is well and good, so long as no one interfered in their perception of what rights and freedoms were.

Climate was getting hot and crops were failing. Food prices were sky-rocketing and everyone who owned a home started refinancing and getting into their retirement plans to survive. They kept telling each other, better days were coming. No one thought to check history. If they had, they would have seen that many times history repeats itself. The majority of this generation hadn't heard of the word depression. Older folks who remembered their grandparents speak of depression really didn't know how to explain to others either. They never experienced this type of poverty before. David shrugged his shoulders as if to shake off the overwhelming thoughts running around his mind.

One cool quiet night as they trudged back to the caves, John said, "David, I noticed you seemed unusually preoccupied all day. Are you doing okay? What's on your mind?" He put his hand on his back and patted it as they walked along the familiar moonlit path. It was so bright that they could see their shadows.

David sighed. "I am so very tired and I wonder if what we are doing is really making any difference. It seems to me that the first couple of months, people were upset that they lost loved ones all around the world." He stopped and faced toward John. "A few people turned to God and repented but the majority didn't. The changes in some are so slight that I feel discouraged."

"Hey, you forget that every time one of those television cameras shows up in front of your face that God's call is going via satellite around the world. We just don't know how many are being affected positively. You'll feel better tomorrow after a good night's rest." John smiled.

Arriving at the caves, the two men were surprised to find the entire group waiting for their return. Pauline grinned, "Welcome brothers, we have a surprise for you! Do you know what tonight is? It's Christmas Eve. Tomorrow is Jesus' birthday." She danced around them and clapped her hands together, excited that she had good news and gifts.

"Yes, God has told us it is time to leave our homes now and live here together. He has told us all independently and today while you were out we began to share with each other what we were being told to do. We have no families left; our loved ones went with Jesus as he called to them. We are just a remnant and so we sold our possessions and will continue to support you in this way until Jesus comes for us. Tonight we shall enjoy a family dinner and tomorrow we will celebrate," Paul echoed her excitement.

David slept fitfully and he was up before dawn. He slipped out of the caves and climbed up the rocks above the city where he wept and prayed. "God I don't understand all these overwhelming emotions. I've always been strong except for Susan." He began to weep again. "I'm feeling so much pain and compassion." He stopped and knelt on the hard rock. "I know there are still more people you desire to come to you. Your people are suffering here, don't you see Lord? How can you let this go on? It's becoming black and white. People are making a decision for or against you. People against you are beginning to loath and ostracize others who are of a different opinion. It is as if love is leaving humanity, they are becoming like animals." David began to pray in groans and crying for God's mercy on the remaining people. He wiped his face with his sleeve of rough sackcloth.

Then suddenly, the sunlight broke through a cloud and God spoke. "My son, you are the one whom I have called to this task. I do indeed see and hear all. Yes, I am love and I have compassion." There was silence in the still air. "However, you must understand that I hate sin. Everyone who will come will come. Everyone must be responsible for his own decisions and actions. I will punish those I love, just as a loving father would punish his children. That way they will not make the same mistake but learn and grow into maturity."

David raised his head to the sky. "Tell me Lord, what am I missing here? I don't understand."

"It's like a mother lion who tells her cubs not go out into the road. What is worse, to disobey and get killed by a big game hunter, or go in the road, come back and his mother gives him a swift hard cuff with her paw? Of course, a hard knock is better than death and hell for eternity. My son, I am angry, my people are becoming worse and more rebellious and disobedient. You know I do not tolerate sin. I promise you, things will become worse on earth. I must get their attention. I have tried to warn the remnant;

only the pure may join me. Help my remaining people, the time is short. This will be their last chance. Soon I will bring you home too precious son." A hot wind began to blow as John continued to hear the voice. "I will tell you something through John so that you might know that I Am, that I Am and be encouraged. I love you and I love your obedient heart. Be strong and go forth. You are one third of the way!"

David fell on his knees and began to praise and worship. He didn't know how long he had been there when John climbed up to get him. "David, David" John shook him. "Are you all right? We have all been looking for you. David, the weirdest thing happened to me on the way to find you. Who is Susan?" John raised his eyebrows and scratched his head.

"She was my wife a long time ago," David moaned. "Why do you ask?"

Because the Lord told me to tell you, you will see her when he calls you home," answered John.

"No way. She died right after I saw her and she not only rejected me, but Jesus as well."

John laughed out loud and grabbed David by the shoulders. "Praise God! That's exactly what the Lord said you would say. He told me to answer you this way; a secret agent who was saved led her to the Lord on her deathbed. Our God reigns. He's still in the business of making miracles. He's also the Creator of human emotions and He understands the hope of millions. Now you can press on the mark, right David?" His friend hugged him so tightly that David could hardly breathe.

David felt he could fly on that good news forever. Nothing he did up until now was in vain. It was with renewed strength and vigor that the two prophets continued their work. News that he would see Susan was the best Christmas present David had ever received. John gave David a pat on the back and led him back to their little family. There was a lot of excitement which flowed among the believers that first Christmas together. Jennifer purchased new sandals for everyone and they enjoyed a wonderful feast. David never liked fish, which became most of their protein. This dinner, however, was special. The women prepared lamb. It was made in the traditional way and so tasty but almost too rich for the little group. They took turns sharing round the table of their experiences the past few months. Everyone had their jobs to do and life, although hard, was exciting. A couple of people in the group had a huge responsibility of picking up the new converts and teaching them the Word. Dailey Bible studies were held at the caves. Many of these people had nowhere else to go. They were the forsaken of the world. They were not good enough, like broken toys, and no longer useful in today's fast-paced society. They lived in a world that was rapidly heading to self-destruction.

Someone in the group brought a small television with them and David managed to get satellite programs and news pulled in. Another brought a computer with all the equipment that went with it, including a printer. The group began asking God to provide someone to repair it. They could see what a great advantage there would be if they could get on-line. David tinkered with it but was at a loss as to what needed to be done.

The New Year was sure to bring answers as the rag-tag group continued to fast and pray. God's call was going around the world in a number of different ways and the Great Commission was being accomplished.

Chapter 35

Year II

    David and John began to get death threats as they preached around the City. At first they came from terrorists but after a year into their ministry, people of other faiths and atheists began to attack. For the most part, God would warn them of any imminent danger and they could avoid or re-create the situations. People were beginning to notice that the two were becoming more powerful with each passing day. Both men knew what the Word foretold about them; however each incident left them amazed. The whole situation felt as if they were watching themselves in action from above rather than living it.

    One day, a madman came screaming at them. He carried a semi-automatic rifle and began firing bullets in rapid succession. Then while being televised around the world, a light came down around the two prophets and the bullets ricocheted off them. They two men pointed their fingers at their attacker and commanded him in the Name of Jesus to leave them alone. Frightened he took a stray bullet in the arm, he dropped the gun and ran away screaming that they were men of God. An hour later, he returned with his arm hanging by his side. He sobbed in their arms, begging their forgiveness and asked them to pray for him. John and David knelt with him on a dusty street and prayed the Sinner's Prayer. "Now brother, you are clean, may your arm be healed in the Name of Jesus Christ of Nazareth?" John prayed.

The man followed them the rest of the day trying to explain to anyone who would listen to him what happened. Several cussed and spat upon him. "What's wrong with these people? Look what has happened to me! Aren't they afraid?" Bloody and dirty he sniffed.

John and David explained that people's hearts were becoming hard and they couldn't hear the Holy Spirit. This man had nowhere to go that night so they took him home and the family adopted him. His name was Peter Johnson and he became a strong prayer warrior for the two prophets.

***

David came back to the caves one evening to share what he and John had seen. Multitudes of people were running around with a mark. It looked like a bar-code. It was on some foreheads, others on their hands. The mark was as varied as were the people. Everyone enjoyed his or her own special design. Some people chose to have an invisible mark upon them. David knew it was coming because of his earlier involvement. A few years before, the mark had been implemented but it was invisible. Now, here it was, in plain sight. People were accepting the mark because it seemed fashionable and in sync. Now, people really knew what others believed. It seemed to have happened overnight. No longer could people, without the mark, barter or trade with others. A final choice was soon approaching. Why just the day before, the Bank of the United States went bankrupt and now the people were given no choice but to plug into the World Banking System.

The world began to visibly fall into a huge state of depression. Desperate people became looters and murderers. World leaders tried to pacify their people by telling them they had been warned and it wasn't too late to join the world. Several world leaders were strong but one stood out among the others promising peace to all if they would calm down and listen to what he said. Stories began trickling around the world that dissenters were being killed. Most of the murders were done by people in underground movements in the middle of the night. Fear continued to grow among the people.

John and David went from place to place begging for people to repent. People mocked them, throwing garbage at them. "So you can save us, huh? Prove it. Where is the rain?"

So the prophets of God raised their hands in Praise. "Send rain Father, your people are thirsty." The heavens broke loose. Torrents of rain came down and great floods began to run. There were basketball sized hailstones. People around the world died as a result of being hit. After many years of drought, there were no plant roots to hold the soil in place. One day it rained blood in various places on the planet. Time after time, the scientific community gave reasons why these events were happening.

One evening, just before sunset, a tiny, dirty, dark haired, seven year old, girl came before John and David, "I have nowhere to go. I want to belong to Jesus; please Sirs help me to find Him. I know He will save me and take me to Heaven." They wept with her and took her to Jennifer and the other women. The ladies wiped her tear streaked face, brushed her hair and introduced her to the Living God. She had a brand new family to love and care for her. They called her their little dove because her heart was so pure.

Another incident happened a few days later when David was being attacked. John stretched his hand forth, pointing his finger, he commanded the camera man of a large TV crew to leave them alone. The man simply dropped dead. Frightened, the crew ran away with the whole scene on tape. Now the men were getting round the world attention as a pair of crazy murderers. To keep the others safe, John and David began to sleep in different areas around the city, rather than to go out to the caves every night. Most people were practicing occult beliefs and a false new world religion so they were afraid that the caves were haunted by the "crazies" as the Jesus people were called.

Much to John and David's surprise one day; they were both whisked away in a cloud of bright light. The time lasted a few minutes and they found themselves in New York City. Another day they were in San Francisco, and yet on the third day, London, England. Then in South Africa reports began coming in of the same incidents. Each trip was the same. They preached repentance and salvation. Many ran to them for prayer and as the day drew to a close, the crowds would become so huge and unruly that the local authorities tried to arrest them for disturbing the peace. Excuses they gave to the people was that since these men caused problems, people's lives were in danger; it was for everyone's protection that they be caught. As the military police laid hands on them, they would vanish, but not before each city had been thoroughly affected. Hail fell and water hydrants broke. Instead of water pouring out of the broken pipes, blood would shoot straight into the air. Biological warfare was unleashed a decade before and the cities were filthy, with no good drinking water. Death was a daily affair. People's normal part of clothing was protective face masks. Many chose to gaily coordinate them with their clothing. Another necessity was to carry stun guns if they could get away with them. The small pen shaped weapons could be easily hidden unless one had to go through a checkpoint or to purchase food. The world was a fearful place during this period.

Many new diseases mutated and science could not keep up with a solid treatment plan, let alone cures. Diseases that hadn't been around for generations were also appearing. Young doctors had never seen the symptoms to make a diagnosis. Smallpox and polio were on the rise again with tuberculosis showing up round the world. Diseases that were once eradicated in the twentieth century were rearing their ugly heads once again.

Praying and fasting together was important to the small community of believers in Jerusalem. David never experienced this type of love and support except for the genuine love and help that the Browns and Lewis' showed him. He often wondered how he made it on earth this long without much fellowship. He knew he could get help of any kind from anyone without judgment. He was amazed as well about his personal growth. His character was changing and he was becoming much more patient with his fellowman. He spoke with John and questioned the changes. He wanted to know how in the world he got in this position. He also wanted to know if it was okay with God to ask Him why things were this way. The answer was affirmative. John being somewhat older, in age, but walking with the Lord most of his life, volunteered some answers and thoughts. The gentle pastor listened to David. He praised God for such a good strong brother to support him as they both tried to obey their Father in heaven. David was learning of the awesome power he had been given in the name of Jesus and in the beginning it frightened him. John, very patiently began showing him scriptures where they were called for a purpose, just like their brothers and sisters back at the caves. They had all been called by the Lord Jesus Christ to share their gifts and talents in love toward and for one another. They were also to love outsiders. Time was short and the tribulation had already past. A tiny remnant remained. Those who would accept Jesus into their lives could still come to Him. "God, please don't let us miss sharing your love with anyone," they all prayed every day.

David was so immersed in what was happening that he hadn't really paid attention when so many people around the world disappeared. He didn't watch much news after his conversion. He began concentrating on reading the Bible. One of the most interesting facts David learned was that his walk with Jesus was a process of growth and maturity. When God looked at him, through the blood of Jesus, he was already fully developed.

One hot dusty afternoon, as the two men took a break in the middle of the street, a man began screaming and running toward them. He was full of fear and although the pair could see no one behind him, they didn't doubt that he was being chased. Nothing came as a surprise to them after a year and a half.

"David, David! Is that you?" An emaciated man fell to his knees sobbing. David seemed to recognize his voice. The human was disheveled, weak and filthy. He was also full of lice and blisters that appeared to be smallpox. David lifted him up and as he stared into his eyes, he believed it was his old computer friend, Frank.

"Frank?" David stopped him as he ran toward him. He grabbed him by his shoulders. As David spoke his name a second time, the feeble man fainted in his arms. "John, we must get him back to the caves. I know him and I fear he may not make it much longer." Back at the caves, they placed him in the care of their fellow believers.

Three days later, the man became coherent and they were able to share the gospel with him and help him clean up. He was still confused about what happened. He remembered two years ago or so, he lost his entire family. "I thought after losing everyone, I would try to retire and get out of the system. I see how hopeless and naïve that was now." Frank was sitting near the fire shivering while he spoke to the group and struggled to tell them what happened to him. He reached toward the fire and rubbed his hands together. "I thought I would try to find David, maybe he would have answers. I wanted enough answers so that I could make plans for myself for the future, then I read the Bible."

David asked, "Well what did you find out about the Bible? John would you pour Frank another cup of coffee? I think he's chilled."

"Thank you John. I learned enough that I was determined not to get the mark. I knew I was in a lot of trouble because I was reminded for the last time. I made plans to find David. I found out where he was and when I got permission under an excuse I made up, they warned me to tell David that he better obey and receive the mark or else."

Jennifer interrupted, "Tell us more...weren't you scared? Sounds like a pretty solid threat. What would have happened a few years back to you?" She handed the man a warm wet cloth to wipe his face and hands.

"Well, I would have been forced or die in the process. It was already happening and David and I knew it was coming. We didn't talk much about it; we were kept busy, so busy in fact that we couldn't do anything but work and fall into bed to start somewhere else in another city, another country all around the world. You can bet I was getting scared." Frank shook off unseen demons and memories. "I thought if I could retire young, I could hide somewhere. Since I was alone, I figured it wouldn't cost much to live. I wanted answers and to drop out of sight, this seemed to be the best way." He brushed his sandy gray hair out of his face and shrugged his shoulders.

Everyone around him mumbled and shared similar stories. "Wow, you really had a rough time getting here didn't you? There seems to be some gaps in what happened. Do you remember when you got to Israel?" Peter looked at him with raised eyebrows and scooted closer to the fire where Frank sat.

"I remember that I was missing my appointments with the world government for the implantation of my identity chip. I needed it to buy a ticket for the plane trip. I got into the computer system and got them off of one of the big-wigs accounts. No one ever keeps track of their budgets." He grinned at having tricked his boss. "Then I got sick and couldn't get out of bed. As my fever rose, I think I must have begun hallucinating. Voices and people started to chase me and I couldn't rest. Even when I fell asleep, things were chasing me." He shared with the group how a bright light appeared one night and told him to run and not accept the chip. Frank coughed deep and raspy, wheezing to regain his breath. He sounded as if any moment there would be none. "I got on the plane in New York; it was a direct flight and felt so chilled and tired." He pulled his new blanket around him and clutched tighter at it as he recalled his horror. "I saw the cold water below me and then somehow, I was standing on the wing looking in the window at myself." He stammered and a puzzled look melted across his face. "There was this voice…it called to me, sounded like my dead grandfather. It was deep and stern but full of love. The voice, it was so real, I didn't have a choice but to obey." It was obvious that the man lost all track of time and there were a lot of blank spaces in his story. Frank continued to struggle to focus on what happened to him for the past two years. "I was found by a kind family. I told them about David and they looked for him. Finally they brought me to Jerusalem and I got lost from them in the crowds. I couldn't see. I guess sand and salt got in my eyes and scratched them. They stung for a long time." Great tears overflowed and ran down out of his eyes onto his cheeks. "All I owned was my dog, and now I've lost him too." He sobbed harder.

"Ah Frank, it will be okay. You are in a safe place. God sent you here, we need to care for you, and we need you to help us with all this outdated computer equipment that we have managed to collect. We love you brother." Paul went to him and held him for a long while as others offered comfort and prayer.

Pauline spoke, "We have some medication with us Frank and I think you need some antibiotics for that cough of yours. It sounds like you still have a lung problem and it may help your immune system and of course, we will pray for you. God uses everything to help his people."

For weeks, he dealt with intense itching as if ants occupied every inch of his body. There were raw open wounds from scratching. He tried to wear socks on his hand at night and the group continued to pray and sought a healing for him. Eventually Frank began to heal, at least emotionally and spiritually. Then he began to look at the computer equipment and see if any repairs could be done. Much to everyone's surprise, one day he broke some codes and began to intersect important world information at a fast pace. He tried to unsuccessfully set up a web site, lacking some pieces to put together one. He did however; tie his system into one satellite dish so that they were able to preach the gospel message around the world. The small band of Christians didn't have a way of knowing how many would receive God's call this way but time was of the essence. Frank was terribly excited that he figured out a way to outsmart the system.

Chapter 36

Once again, Jennifer came through with Christmas gifts for all. Some wonderful food with praise and worship made for one of the best Christmas's many of the new converts enjoyed in many years.

That Christmas Eve, David began to share with the group, "My dear sisters and brothers, not all of us have all knowledge of future events, which is the beauty of scripture; we can rely on God's Word for the answers. I feel a foreboding and the hunger in me grows intense as we get the Truth out. Our planet is in trouble and the people are truly turning into animals. If you think it has been hard the last fifty years or so, I assure you, it will become worse. Brother will attempt to betray brother and please do not think that each is exempt. God will return as He has promised." He sighed. "I know you say to yourselves that He tarries, but He longs for that one last sheep. The Word tells us in the Book of Revelations that it is approximately three and one-half years that John and I have to preach. That would be forty-two months or one thousand two hundred sixty days. The outer court has been given to the Gentiles and our beloved city is being trampled. The wickedness of the Gentiles is unrestrained." David took a deep breath and held up his thumb and forefinger. "My point is, precious ones, we roughly have one and one-half years before we go. The Word tells us that at that point, the Seventh Trumpet will be blown. Things will undoubtedly become worse in the next year."

John spoke up, "Yes, beloved ones, Psalm 79:1, Isaiah 63:18, and Luke 21:24 all confirm -what David is telling you. You dressed us with sackcloth two years ago as we came to you. The attire was prophetic and pointed us as to what we were supposed to do. Now I know you are all having a rough time making ends meet. Yet, God has blessed us all with miracle after miracle. You must understand that our bodies, humanly speaking are being taxed and as the future unfolds, we all must go to be with the Father." He half-smiled. "I know how David and I will pass; however, I'm unable to speak for each of you. You must not become discouraged or lose faith as we each move forward into the realm of heaven. My prayer is that you continue to praise and thank the Lord for His mighty works." He caught people's eyes as he glance around the group and acknowledge them with love. "At each death, we must celebrate the good fortune of our precious soul mates and rejoice with the angels. They welcome us as they help us. So take courage, for your redeemer draws nigh. Don't become fearful dear friends. Look up and keep your eyes on Jesus! I share this because we all know that our time is so very short." The group began to pray even harder.

That night, Frank went to be with the Lord. Then, the fellow believers began to fast and pray for the Lord's strength to hear His voice in their hearts even more. They also prayed that they would carry out their assigned purposes to the best of their abilities.

Day after day, the exhausted pair went out into the world. When the two men returned, their small group would have refreshments ready and share the latest information about the city. There would be updates on the equipment and what they learned on world news from the computer. Reports from the ones who left the caves to gather food or other necessities were shared. Some computer parts were wearing out so they were not always aware of the rapid deterioration of the world as were John and David. A lot depended on where God sent them.

Each day, they became more powerful and people grew more afraid of them. One incident in Singapore happened when the two called out a plague of roaches. The entire story was sent around the world on the world news station at a rapid. Another day, in Africa, the same type of plague but it was frogs that came forth. In Anchorage, Alaska they called heat and lightening from the sky. The heat was so intense; it began to melt glaciers and caused the sea to rise at an alarming rate. Many people died in each case. Scientists were trying to explain things to people using weather causes. They broadcast not only through daily news but weather channels, history channels, and world public channels. However, by the end of the third year, a lot of people were not satisfied with scientific answers. They believed that these two men were definitely in the way of their health and happiness. They were finally getting used to an OWG and as long as they were not fighting for their lost freedoms, the system left them alone. Those who suspected anything different were immediately disposed of. No one asked questions, no one knew, nor did they want to know. People began to wonder why there were few citizens over the age of fifty. They were being told that most illnesses killed older people and that diseases were less and that accounted for less sick people. Some people thought it was odd that if there were less people getting sick, then what was happening to the older ones. People were afraid to voice their thoughts. Almost all diseases that were left, according to the system, were fatal. Some of the older people refused to go to the hospitals. Most of the folks, when they got there, did not return. Fear, once again became even more intense than in previous years. Bodies were piling up and incinerators were being built because of few, but highly contagious diseases.

As time progressed, the small band of Christians began to go home to be with the Lord. David and John were relieved as each one that passed away did not suffer but gave up their spirit in their sleep. Many fell asleep singing and praising, waking the others as they departed.

The summer proved to be intensely hot in the Holy city and the outer-court of twenty-six acres had been given to the Gentiles for a big amusement park, complete with cool, water recreational, activities. The Lord directed John and David to go there and preach. "Repent, repent," they cried as they walked about. Most people spat upon them and told them to leave them alone. All of a sudden, the water stopped running down the slides. Then it came on again, hot, and blood began to come out of the spigots and fountains. People became angry and soon a riot started with John and David in the middle. They started to mock them and threw stones trying to hit the two men. John and David went to the concert stage where they begged the crowd of uncontrollable people to listen to them. As they threw stones, trash, clothing, glass bottles, and food, John and David started throwing flames of fire back, breaking things in the air. Glass and all types of debris came raining down upon crowds. Soon the military arrived, firing bullets at the two men. Bullets were deflected and ricocheted back into the crowd of unprotected bodies. All of a sudden the two men disappeared into thin air. No one could find them. OWG began to realize that if they didn't get rid of these two, they would lose control. A demand ransom was decreed and sent around the world. The world had yet to realize this was a spiritual battle. The Word was clear about this one.

A long and hard year followed, but John, David and the

group served one another well and continued to encourage each other. They lost many soldiers by the time Christmas came again.

Chapter 37

Year III

There were seven individuals left from last Christmas. They were a rag-tag bunch. They missed Jennifer because she had such talent for meeting each material need. Little Dove was blessed with a gifted voice and unconditional hugs and she was gone too. Everyone that was gone was missed.

The remaining few were excited about the upcoming six months and although there was an element of unknown fear, praise and worship strengthened each individual.

"What's that noise sounds like whimpering?" John raised his eyebrows.

"Ahh," everyone chorused as a little dog bounded out into the middle of the group. "I found her behind one of the restaurants and decided to hide her behind me for a Christmas present for all of you." David giggled.

"Isn't she cute?" Everyone chorused together. The little golden retriever puppy ran from face to face licking them and wriggling all over. As she grinned from ear to ear, she made the entire group laugh.

"I've named her Lucky Lady," David said. "Now that our faces are cleaned, I suggest that we wash one another's feet. Do we have enough water?"

"Yes, we do," answered one of the women. "The well behind us is still producing the freshest water in the area."

There was a small juniper tree with twinkling lights that someone found in a trash heap and John attempted to play a flute that one of the men left behind. The grateful group enjoyed a night and day of rest and peace while they played with their new present.

Chapter 38

John and David stank as they trudged back to the empty caves. They were the remaining two of the group who left to be with Jesus last Easter Sunday morning. Their little dog slowly wagged her tail and followed the men. They could not have asked for a more faithful companion.

"You know David, I feel something oppressive. I've lost track of the days, but I know it's been about three months since Easter and but for the "Grace of God", we should have been dead long ago."

"Yes," David answered. "I feel it as well. We have enough food for the three of us for a week or so and we've had a lot of close calls lately. I've also lost track, but one thing I know is...let's prepare our bodies. I am prepared spiritually." He brushed the dust off his clothing as they walked down the dirt path. "I just want anyone who will listen to accept the truth and bring glory to His Holy Name."

The evening brought clean baths. They tried to rinse out their dark sackcloth. They could not shave because their dull razor cut them and their sandals were worn out from many miles of use.

Their hair was long and grey. They were two dried up old irritants who were hated by the world.

David woke before the sun came up to find John missing. He gave a whistle for Lady and they went looking for their friend. After an hour or so, they found him in exactly the same place as David was three and one-half years ago.

John was on his knees with his head buried in his hands. As he looked at his fresh licked hand and then up to David, he continued to weep. "This was such a beautiful city at one time. So many of God's children lived here and I know the time is short. The lost are so lost and there will be no one to stand in the gap. My heart is broken. I feel faint-hearted. I also feel like...what is all this for? What if this is a stupid joke and everything is in vain?" He raised his arms in the air above him and shook his head. "What if we're wrong David? What if we really are crazy? My faith is very weak David. I don't know what I'm here for. I haven't been able to lead anyone to Christ since Easter and you know what? I loved Jennifer." he admitted. "Nothing came of my feelings but I miss her and her little boy Dave so much. She was so strong. I used to fantasize that this was all a bad dream and when the world got better, we could get married and maybe have a family." He broke into fresh sobs. "What if all we have done is some type of trickery?"

This time it was David's turn to be strong. "John, get hold of yourself and your thoughts. You must not forget no matter how many times God has used us supernaturally that we are only humans made in His image." He put his arms around John's shoulders to comfort him. "We still have to deal with our humanness until we are called home." David gulped, "Do you remember me telling you about that night in the hotel room when Satan came after me? He dumped confusion and self-doubt on me. I had to pray hard and rebuke him. It's okay to have those feelings about Jennifer and Dave. They are natural human longings. God made you a man." David grimaced; John's comments stirred his own memories of Susan. He drew a circle in the soil with his toe and a cross attempting to distract his mind. "Now friend, let's pray together."

They prayed all morning. As they walked back to the caves to refresh themselves, Lady stepped on a thorn and they carried her back with them. She apologetically lay down on a cool stone in the cave and stayed there.

"What if we don't come back?" John looked up as he bent down to pet her.

David grinned, "I suspect God will take care of her. After all, he brought her to us right?"

"But... John argued, "Animals aren't supposed to go to heaven."

"I believe they will be there and besides John, that's God's problem. No way, I'm not going to put God into a box after all that we've been through. Think about it, there are animals in the Bible and God made everything good. The Almighty will take care of our Lady." He put his hand out to John and helped him stand up.

Chapter 39

The Jerusalem Diner

Joe yawned and tapped on his silver military watch as he observed the diner across the street. Multicolored neon lights flashed along the top of the aluminum roof. A green one flickered weakly as it blinked to keep up with the others. The diner was pretty and magical in the Thomas Kinkaid sense of the word. It looked nostalgic, built two centuries ago in the early 1900's. One could only guess how many times it was refurbished over the years.

The morning star appeared on a bright horizon and everything looked surreal in the early dawn.

Joe's bulging muscles rippled and tightened as he noticed every movement in the grey light. Shadows played against the buildings with the rising sun. He pushed back his night goggles and brushed sandy-brown hair out of his dirty crusty face. His intense blue eyes darted about the scene before him.

Soon Joe would be off his midnight shift. He was bone tired and glad this assignment was almost finished. His

Assignment: A special unit guard for two bodies that lay in front of him. This became a lot more that what he anticipated. He was close to retirement after many years of this special work. Joe was trained as a global investigator and detective. He was in a unique position in the One World Government.

Joe worked for what the world once knew as the United Nations. Now, he answered only to the leader of the OWG. A big argument ensued among the nations as to what they wanted to call themselves. They believed they needed to find something worthy to represent the Earth because soon they would be meeting up with extra-terrestrial beings. He didn't care to be involved in world politics. The whole reason he wanted to be there was to protect the people.

***

Reporters crawled all over the place and people rejoiced over these two dead men that lay in front of Joe. The fifty year old officer and his comrades were assigned to this military mission to protect the corpuses from citizens who were celebrating their deaths. It was a crazy scene. He observed something similar decades ago, called Mardi Gras in New Orleans, Louisiana in the United States. People went wild partying. Colorful streamers and necklaces flew in the air and frenzied partygoers grabbed them as they exchanged gifts. At last, the people of earth were relieved of having to no longer listen to "false ideas."

These two men caused all types of confusion and arguments when they were alive. They were difficult to keep track of over the last three and one-half years, but Joe knew they and their comrades lived out in the caves and burial grounds. Local people were superstitious and would not go out there. The tomb dwellers could do all kinds of tricks and Joe's orders were to let the little band of renegades alone because soon they would all die anyway. They didn't bother his global leader but they did annoy people. They seemed to convict others and make them feel that they were responsible for themselves and their freedom of choice. They were teaching false ideas about a savior who would rescue them, Jesus was his name. These people rebelled against receiving the laser mark on their bodies. Everywhere they went, they would do some type of exciting event that some called miracles and get the public all wound up. Explosive outbursts happened regularly. There would be arguments and controversy and then Joe and his Special Forces Unit would have to go in and quiet things back down and assure the citizens. The man's job was tough. Things weren't getting any easier and for some reason, these two men could move their bodies supernaturally all over the earth. It was hard to catch them.

    Joe's leader depended on him and never really interfered with what he tried to do. He gave Joe free rein but…was often watched. Joe suspected that was the case but it didn't bother him because he did nothing to cause his Commander to believe differently.

    One afternoon, just as the leader predicted, the last person in the little band of resistors died. Joe knew because he overheard a radio transmission from one of the local vendors who was selling food to them although they didn't have the proper identification. Now, the two leaders of the group were left and Joe was observing them.

***

    Sometime in the spring, around what the rag-tag Christian group declared as Easter, Joe saw two men appear in the streets of Jerusalem. The day was bright and clear and the wind was calm. The smell of spring was floating about and people seemed preoccupied with their usual business transactions in the city streets. Vendors quibbled over prices and exchanges were made. No one could buy or barter without the unseen tattoos on their bodies. Only a laser could pick up the mark and the latest scanner was the most sought-after new technical piece of equipment one could purchase in the 21st century.

Joe knew the two men to be John and David. They were called many names, mostly derogatory. The world seemed to hate them because everywhere they went David and John were associated with rioting and trouble. This morning they were different. They were cleaned up and their ragged clothes were spotless. The men were barefoot and their long grey beards were washed and combed. Long time irritants and useless old fools, they arrived at the designated spot and began to preach about Big Brother and a One World System. The majority of Jerusalem ignored them except the television crews crawling all over with their commentators ready to predict and explain their every move. Why were they so clean today? Is there a new twist to what they have to say? The reporters went on and on with their babbling and insistent questions.

***

Big Brother observed from his office and shrugged his shoulders most of the time, but today was different. It was time to finish them off. Why not kill them in front of the television crews so that the whole world could watch? He could convince the world that these two were not infallible and only human like the rest of them. Forget this silly stuff about being made in the image of God and Jesus returning for His people. The rag tag group died off three months ago and most of the stories of Jesus returning were explained scientifically. This talk of people rising over three years ago was in the past and people were so busy working for a living that there was no time to do anything else. The citizens' lives consisted of work, indoor gyms with pools, and midnight news. There was only one news channel and that was the World News Station. This scene could be so well implemented that it would surely discourage any other uprising in the name of freedom of speech, right, etc. Big Brother laughed to himself, "crushed finally and forever." Soon he would have total control over his domain.

***

Shots rang out in the balmy air startling several birds. As they took flight upwards, David and John fell in the dusty city streets of Jerusalem. No one knew where the shots came from although camera crews scrambled to pan around the area, there was no one to be found. There was much speculation; the final surmise was that the shooter was a disgruntled, mentally unbalanced person.

Joe and his unit were already there in the shadows. They moved in quickly forcing the crowds and news people away from the still forms before them.

The crowd went crazy and a celebration started immediately. Everyone began spreading the word that their irritants were dead and they were free to do as they pleased. No more criticizing of their lifestyles. The One World Leader declared a day of observance and employers were ordered to let their people have the day off. The scene echoed throughout the world. Between eating and drinking, everyone watched the television screens with live coverage from their satellite systems. No one was ignorant as to what happened.

"Move back." Joe motioned with his arms towards the nearest camera crews.

"Watch out." Someone shouted in the crowd as a woman was knocked to the ground by retreating reporters. The crowd roared as they realized what really happened.

Joe briefed his team before they went in and now began to give directions moment by moment. He quickly divided the team of six men into three teams of two and they broke into military day, swing, and mid-shifts. The entire six stayed together the first day and then began the watch change over the second morning.

"We must be careful," he cautioned his men. "There are going to be bounty hunters and all types of characters out here. One piece of hair or anything off these bodies will sell for a fortune. Sean and I will take the midnight shift because the camera crews won't be so alert. Daytime will be less of a danger because of the television catching more shots of people and it will be harder for them to get close to the bodies.

The first mid-shift became busy as people prepared to camp out, especially the news reporters. Joe and his team put a makeshift electric fence around the bodies. A yellow barbed wire ran six feet around the perimeter of the two slain men. It was powerful enough to throw a human off his feet and daze him for a few minutes until a soldier could drag him off. Several people did not heed the warning signs and found themselves in a back alley, dazed and suffering from a headache the rest of the day. There were colorful streamers and balloons all over the streets and a parade was scheduled for the following day as different characters emerged from the shadows of fear and quiet in the city.

"Those blasted news reporters are getting on my nerves," Joe growled. He pushed a couple of them out of the way as he tried to cover one of the bodies with the blanket that blew off in a little dust devil.

"Take it easy Joe, you're tired. These reporters don't mean any harm; they are just trying to do their job. Actually they are doing well from what I hear from the Commander. He is pleased with the amount of attention and circulation going on all over the world." Sean wiped his brow. "I'll be glad when our shift is over."

He offered Joe a drink from his canteen.

"Ah, there you are." Joe stretched out his hand and shook with the new team arriving for shift exchange. "People seem to be quieting down, it's near dinner time and as you can see there are campers all over the place, but it's mostly news crews." He sniffed the air full of good barbeque smells from the campfires. "Hmm, I'm getting hungry."

"Hello Joe and Sean. We will take it from here. Get some rest and see you around midnight. By the way, the Commander wants a briefing and he has some plans he wants to share with Joe before you settle in. Team one is resting now and will relieve you in the morning." The older soldier smiled and shook their hands again.

***

"Yes Sir, Sean and I have control over the bodies and the news people are being respectful. Do you wish us to give them a briefing?" Joe stood at full military attention in the office of his quiet strong Commander. He was showered and wore clean camouflage clothing.

"No I don't think that will be necessary. I plan to have a full report that I will give the World Secretary to read at about noon tomorrow. I will be out of town and this will work with my plan perfectly. I do want the presence of your team all around for that moment though." He grinned and rubbed his hands together. "Make sure you are all dressed in full war uniform with your weapons. It is nice and intimidating. I want people to understand what a danger these two men were and how efficient we are at protecting them from any gimmicks or tricks the people might be afraid of."

Joe nodded and saluted. He knew the fear tactics that his commander implemented in the past.

"Well what did he say?" Sean said.

"Just the usual, except that he wants the whole team down there by noon tomorrow so that the Secretary can make an announcement of peace and comfort."

"That's just great. When are we supposed to keep the teams rested?" Sean folded his arms across his chest and frowned.

"Don't even try to understand that Sean, you know this happens all the time." Joe yawned. They were already short on sleep. They would get about six hours before it was time to take the midnight shift.

The second day after the two men had been killed; all the news reporters were told to be ready for a big announcement around noon. People were breathless as they all crowded around water coolers and television sets to hear what Big Brother said about the past day's events.

***

"Good afternoon ladies and gentlemen. It is with regret that our World Leader could not be here but he asked me to speak these words to you." Fluffing her red hair and clearing her throat, the World Secretary began to read an obvious hand written document to the people.

"I share your joy, people of the World, in the death of these two mosquito terrorists. They were indeed the most dangerous known men in the modern world. They and their little band were such an unwelcome intrusion in our peace loving lives. As you may or may not have known, the last of their renegade band died sometime back. We were on the path of destroying these two remaining but someone has taken care of it for us. We do have an on-going investigation but it was probably some crazed person who felt guilty at what they had to say and did the job for all of us. No longer will you live in fear and doubt as to what these people were up to. You have all been good citizens and followed the laws of your government as previous generations have taught you. As you can see, the world is much safer having received the mark put upon you and it wasn't some awful brand as you were thinking. Don't most of you like your personal choices of lovely tattoos, little fairies, elves, dollar signs, they have been limitless and only you can see them. No longer do you have to be afraid of losing your identity. We can find your lost children. People can't get into your bank accounts and travel is once again safe and open to all. You can travel anywhere in the world as you like and don't have to carry your money or identity." The Secretary paused. Then she put her hand on her chest and shook her head in a grateful humble way and waited for her emotion to pass. With a deep breath, she continued. "How much simpler can it get? Just wave your hand over a little wand and you are on your way. A One World Government isn't so bad now is it?"

"You go girl." Someone in the crowd shouted out and they all began to cheer and clap.

The World Secretary added, "We have so much to be thankful for our wonderful leader in these times in history, don't you all agree?" She smiled, stepped back from the makeshift podium, and smoothed the skirt of her white and gold suit.

The crowd went wild and people threw whatever they were holding into the air.

"I'm glad that's over; now let's get back to bed for a few more hours." Joe stretched and yawned.

The two men waved to their comrades and they headed back to the barracks as Joe steered a little lost girl to her mother and placed her in her mother's arms. This exceptional unit of men didn't miss anything. They were always on guard for any unusual movement or sound. In this case the girl was alone and crying.

***

The third night was riddled with silencers who found their victims. The robbers and thrill seekers were getting braver. It was possible that as time wore on, the night guards would not be as alert. Every time that Joe or Sean hit someone, the military quickly moved in to take away the body. The new night goggles were twice as effective. Joe and Sean could see the stalkers before they could see them. Big Brother always believed that no show, no tell was best. The less people knew the better for the government. So except for relatives, no one knew what happened to missing people. The best excuse that he ever came up with was that the person died in the line of duty to the people. The remaining relatives would receive a little medal and a small pewter box with his or her ashes and that was the end of things. No one questioned anymore and that is what Big Brother liked.

"Hello boys, sure glad you're here. It's been one hard night. I think we got rid of at least a dozen troublemakers," Joe said. The sky was dark and quiet as a stealth fighter. Sneaky people were off their guards and didn't know what hit them until it was too late. There were so many it seemed as if they were chasing rats which scampered about, boldly increasing, in numbers, making work more difficult. Joe and his partner were glad to see the team

Sean grinned, "Joe isn't kidding. I wonder when we are going to be able to get rid of those two bodies. It's been three days now and they're becoming fruity." He wrinkled his nose.

One of the guards answered, "Talk is going around that our Commander is planning some type of burning ceremony as soon as things die down."

Joe said, "I hear yesterday got quieter and people were starting to get bored with the same old news. I imagine he'll come up with something. I hope soon because the nights are getting pretty intense. We saw all kinds of beggars, stalkers, and robbers last night. Some were pretty scary too. Thank goodness for these new night goggles. I don't think they knew what hit them."

Zzzzzip, zizzzip... A flashing neon green light exploded and hit the night sky. All four men looked up across the street to see the Jerusalem Diner lights go out. Different colors struggled to come back on and soon they did, except the green one.

"Sean, I think I'm going over to have breakfast this morning before turning in, care to join me?"

"No thanks Joe. I'm exhausted. Keep your ears open, it'll probably be a good place to catch some interesting conversation. Funny, some places never change over the years and this is one of them. A person can find one in almost every major city. Like the heartbeat of a city, know what I mean?" Sean stretched his arms and switched his weapon to the other side of his back. Shoulders hunched, he lumbered away, half asleep. "See you later."

***

Streams of sunlight broke the morning clouds as Joe climbed the steps of the Diner. The screen door creaked giving away its age when Joe opened it. The interior was dark and quiet with just a handful of people inside. They were sleepy regulars that finished a midnight shift or early risers getting ready to go to work.

"Hi Joe, it's been a long time. I've been watching you since I came to work this morning. You guys have been working hard out there. What'll you have, besides a cup of coffee?" A Marilyn Monroe look alike, pulled an order book from her apron pocket and a pen from her wavy, flipped up, blond hair. She smacked her gum and scribbled Joe's order. "Coming right up." She grinned, patted her hair, and spun away.

"Thanks Sally." Joe smiled to himself about this happy person and shook his head at the same time. He hadn't been in but half-dozen times, yet she remembered him and what he liked. Joe wasn't used to anything that had to do with personal attention. She was refreshing as she flirted with everyone who walked through the door.

He shivered every time the squeaky screen door opened and closed from morning traffic. He noticed that the back blue booth was empty and he let out a sigh of relief as he slid into the big leather bench next to the heater. It was a cozy place. Joe could close his eyes for a moment if he liked and he could also be more observant if something warranted attention. Someone left the morning paper on his table and he looked at the front headlines which screamed for attention.

The newspaper was biased as the OWG checked everything before it went to press. A lot of the time, there were press releases written by the World Secretary. This morning there was information on missing persons. Not much, just that some people had been reported as such. Approximately once a week, there was a list of some missing persons and those few found were honored in the paper as "helpers" of the people. Joe was most interested in what was written about the two men lying just outside in the street. He could see everything from where he sat.

The sun was up now as Sally brought him a huge platter of bacon and eggs. There was orange juice, toast, and hash browns. She poured him a second cup of coffee and left the remainder of the pot for him to help himself. Pleased that the owners kept a menu of good old fashioned food, Joe started to eat.

He noticed that the paper disclosed these two men's names. Most people already knew them from all the world exposure. Joe read that there were last names assigned to them in this article. They seemed to be old Christian names. John and David were adequate names at this time for all purposes.

The waitress returned an hour later to find that Joe was snoozing and she placed her oversized soft black sweater around his shoulders, careful not to wake him.

Joe jumped and then fell into a deeper sleep. He was playing in his grandmother's back yard. She laughed and picked up a black book. When her Terrier puppy began to tire from all the fetching, Joe went for a drink of water and came down to sit next to her.

"What are you reading Grandma?"

"I try to read in the Bible every day Joe. It's a good book to read and I find a lot of comfort in it, especially since Grandpa has passed on."

"Where did he pass to?" Joe wrinkled his brow.

"You're young honey, but I'm sure you can understand. Grandpa is in Heaven. God made people and He sent His son Jesus to die for us so we could go to Heaven and join Him and our loved ones forever."

Joe became curious and picked up the Bible from time to time as he grew up but couldn't seem to get interested, after he went to college and ran into so many different opinions. He, like many people, found it easier to listen to everyone else rather than to make any decisions on his own. He was a strong self-made military man who touted a brilliant career. He didn't have much to say one way or another. The main goal in life was to help others enjoy peace and love. The best way Joe knew how to do that was to be a good public servant. His intelligence landed him in this position.

Joe mumbled in his seat and then drifted back again to a time when his Grandmother told him a story about the end times and of two prophets in the Bible. She warned him of the mark of the beast and that these two prophets would make an impact on the world. He questioned her when and where it would happen. She shook her head and reminded him to be ready and on guard when he saw these things taking place in the world. Joe made no connection, confused in his youthful understanding of what her attempts to tell him were.

Joe was raised in the Catholic faith and often silently crossed himself before whispering grace before meals. It was a subconscious motion of gratitude, but he was cautious as many others were in this time in history. He longed for the Universal Church to take its full rightful place in people's lives, but he didn't understand what that meant. There was much talk of a One World religion.

***

The early lunch crowd rushed into the diner all at the same time, rowdy and wound-up as usual. Late events always caused great excitement among them and they all seemed to have a different version of the stories. Updates flew about fast and furious and arguments ensued. Someone bumped into Joe as he grabbed for the paper lying on his table. Joe woke with a jump and hit the coffee pot dumping hot coffee onto his lap.

He excused himself from Sally and a young executive in a black suit that placed himself in the empty booth across from him. They both apologized and attempted to wipe the mess up from the red checkered oilcloth and off Joe. In the washroom, Joe cleaned up. He threw his head back and let the refreshing water run down his neck as he splashed it upward into his face and hair. He blew his nose and dried off, and now wide awake, he returned just as Sally poured him a fresh cup of coffee and offered him lunch.

"No thanks." He smiled warmly and continued, "What's this ruckus about? Every table is full and everyone is talking."

"This is the usual lunch crowd Joe. They're young and excited all the time. There's talk from some of the college students that are from University in the city. They say this recent incident is some type of prophecy of the New Testament. Of course, they don't know what they are talking about. Everybody has a different opinion and everyone thinks they have the correct answer. This group is always debating something." She rolled her eyes and put her hands on her hips. "The latest of course, those two bodies out there..." She turned slightly toward the window and motioned her hand toward the silent forms that lay in the street.

Joe shook his head in agreement. He'd been assigned riot control on several occasions when college students downtown got out of hand. He thought he'd listen in. Perhaps he could pick up on some dissenters that would be helpful to him in the future.

A thin woman chewed on a twisted piece of her brunette hair and argued vehemently with her classmates. "You don't know what you're talking about."

"That's your passion, Gwen; Bible fables. Why don't you make a career of writing children's books? Just because you think that maybe you have run into some truth of old world history, don't push it down our throats." A young man with a blue backpack sat next to her and argued back.

She snapped, "Well Rick, you haven't even taken the class yet, so how come you're going after me? Why don't you try reading your World History Book and catch up with the rest of us?"

Rick whined, "I don't have to, it isn't a requirement for what I need to graduate in Journalism. I need what is current, up to date interviewing, and reporting on what I observe now." He smirked and folded his arms across his chest.

Gwen rolled her eyes. "Then don't go after what you don't read for yourself. Quit making decisions on what you hear instead of considering the facts. That is, if there are any real facts in history books or classes now days.

"Well, I don't like history," Rick protested. "It's too boring."

***

Joe heard another conversation and strained to listen carefully.

An attractive blond woman sat in the booth across the aisle

from Joe, apparently with her employer. They were both well dressed and appeared to be in the legal profession based on their vocabulary. "Did you hear about all the missing people last night?" She leaned toward the man and whispered.

"What do you mean?" An expensively dressed gentleman flipped out his checkered napkin and laid it across his lap, then fiddled with his silverware.

"I have received at least three phone calls from families this morning asking us to take on their cases. It seems all three have the same story; soldiers came to their homes at about two this morning to report deaths of their loved ones. Not only that, but they told them, that they were in the line of duty. No more information was given and no bodies. Their families didn't even know that their relatives were in the "line of duty." She took a sip of coffee and dabbed the corner of her mouth with her napkin. "I'm glad you chose to come here for lunch, I wasn't comfortable sharing this idea in the places we usually go."

He sighed, "Well, I guess we will just have to do what we have to do. String them along for awhile and let's keep their charges to a minimum. It's possible to fight the government and I still haven't found a way to make the living relatives understand how expensive it can become. These people don't have the funds to do this. Let's just appease them for a short time and work on them to drop their cases because there are no leads. I am almost feeling, what is that word? Oh yes, guilty because of the poor suckers." He took a bite from his club sandwich.

"Mister Denton, I think I can come up with some type of form letter that could work. Would you like for me to try? I bet we are going to get more of these claims. We have had several in the past. Maybe we can create a table with a set percentage of their total yearly salary." She smiled and added, "We can work with them until they are short on funds and then come up with some legal jargon that will satisfy them."

"That's not a bad idea, Julie. I rather fancy the thought. There could be some buck in there for us and we are doing them a favor by taking them on and helping with their closures. It isn't like highway robbery and there's that old saying that "you get what you pay for." I know a couple of businesses in town that take people for all they're worth." The attorney looked at his watch. "It's time to go, work on that idea and see what you can come up with." He grinned and patted her arm.

Joe made a mental note to keep an eye on this couple. He knew the man as a type of DA and what they were saying wasn't legal at the moment. He could get some good information on him before he retired.

He looked outside observing his fellow guards and the still bodies. One of them wiped his brow and coughed from the dusty heat rising upwards. The crowds were milling about with cameras. A camel stopped, lay down in the middle of the street, and groaned. People became upset with the animal because he was so large he blocked their view of the dead men. Joe rubbed his eyes because he thought that he noticed one of the bodies move. A breeze picked up and the hair fluttered about the face. By now Joe was wide awake and he glanced at the guard nearest the fence, nothing seemed unusual.

There was so much noise in the crowded diner that everything began to rush together into one big sound in the soldier's ears, like a huge tidal wave. It swept over Joe and took his breath away. He looked around and all of a sudden, he saw everything slow into a motionless time warp. Everyone's mouths were open but there was no sound or movement coming from them.

At once there was a flash of light inside the door at the front of the diner. A huge being appeared to go through the screen door and into the building. He was dressed all in white and a golden light poured from his body. Joe blinked; this being had of all things...what appeared to be wings. The presence turned and looked in all directions. He made eye contact with Joe and began to move toward the startled man.

Joe reacted fast drawing his weapon upward from his side. He pointed it at the fast approaching stranger.

"Shhh." The form put his finger to his mouth and started to speak. "I am not here to hurt you. I have come for John and David. Be still and know who my Lord is. See what He will do according to the Scriptures of old."

"Who are you?" Joe blinked again because the light was so brilliant and the being was the most beautiful thing that he could ever remember seeing. It didn't seem to want to hurt him. The voice was gentle, yet commanding so Joe put his gun down. He was more in awe than afraid of what this stranger might do.

"My name is Michael; I am an archangel and one of God's messengers. Jesus is with me today. We have come for God's faithful prophets. God always has someone on Earth to spread his Word. These two men are servants of the Most High God, Supreme Commander of the World." His eyes burned with liquid love and demanded the startled man to pay attention. "It is foretold that we would come for these precious ones. The truth is in the Word of God."

"What is the Word of God?" Joe said.

The angel sighed, "The Bible is the infallible Word of God. If only the people would read it instead of depending on a man to have all the answers." His eyes were piercing as he continued, "They have become lazy and complacent."

The soldier said, "Why are you speaking to me only, there are a million people out there and everyone is still, even the people inside don't seem to know you are here?"

Michael grew brighter and stood taller, "The day has arrived for you to prepare to meet your maker, it is not God's will that anyone should perish but all have everlasting life. God has seen your confusion and honored your request to become His and save you."

Joe was astounded. "When did I do that?"

"Why don't you remember? When you were a child, you sat on your Grandmother's lap after your Grandfather died. You cried and cried because he was such a strong influence in your life, full of love; especially after your own father passed away so young. You missed him a lot. Your Grandmother introduced you to Jesus and you prayed with her. You have never spent much time with Him but you never turned away either. You struggled to obey the Ten Commandments that she taught you." The huge angel looked down at the small man below his waist and smiled. "Many times you've been protected by one of us or your assigned Guardian as you grew up. You were often in awe of some wonderful thing in your life that you couldn't explain. I'm here now explaining to you. God has come for the last of His believers in a rebellious world. He will continue in another time and place with all of you."

"But..."

"Hush now. We have to finish what we came for. Follow me." Michael began to move backward toward the door.

Joe obeyed his direction and followed the huge angel out through the screen door of the blinking diner. Red lights sputtered, on their way to burning out next. The people started to mill about as Joe was hit, the shot placed straight into his heart. His body fell in slow motion down the steps of the Jerusalem Diner. He knew it was the World Commander himself that pulled the trigger and placed his body inside the perimeter of marked electric wire.

He saw the noisy crowd become quiet as they all looked up because an unseen voice called out, "Come up!" At once a whirlwind dropped out of the sky. Out of a large twister, Jesus appeared through parting black clouds. His presence was strong and commanding as well. Joe could feel his body rise to his knees and he began to worship. "Jesus," he cried out and tears ran down his hardened face as he recognized a person he had seen so long ago when he lost his Grandfather.

"Don't leave me behind." He pleaded as he crossed himself.

"*A sincere cry from a repentant heart never goes unheard.*" Joe's heart received the message with great joy although no one else heard the thought or outward voice.

The two bodies before Joe rose through a bright tunnel of flooding light in obedience to the command given them. The tough soldier raised his hands upward in praise and worship, suddenly finding himself caught in the light and following the two men through unmistakable smoke and the smell of incense.

Joe looked down through the tunnel and saw the people watching. He moved like the blink of an eye, but underneath him, life was motionless and he could see his fellow guards still standing up on the wooden platforms that were around the outside of the wire fence. They were in place ready to fire but were unable to do so. He felt sorry for them because he knew that they would be killed when this was over. They hadn't done their job, just as he hadn't, so he was shot by someone or something with supernatural power as he came through the door. He now understood how spiritual and evil the World Commander was.

Joe smiled; he was going to see Grandfather. Oh, how he missed him over the years. Maybe he would take him fishing.

Chapter 40

Shots rang out in the heavy afternoon air, killing John and David. They fell down in the middle of the streets in Jerusalem. There was television crews from every satellite connected to the world system. Big Brother was on top of everything. Big Brother set an obvious trap from which there was no escape. The two men didn't know what hit them. People were disappointed that there wasn't more of a big showdown. It didn't make any difference because the news hyped things up and re-ran this event for hours on end.

John and David's death was not in vain. A world that remained would still not listen. God in all of His mercy and patience was indeed sad. Freedom to choose was what He gave the human race.

A worldwide holiday was declared by the world leader who gleefully spread the wonderful news that the world's mosquitoes were deceased and the people could go about their business without harassment. There would be no more threats and silly tricks in the air.

People began to party and exchange gifts with each other.

They gathered together in neighborhoods at the end of the workday, sharing their evening meals. With striking conversations, they observed the latest newscasts on their big satellite television screens. Their pride rose as a stench in God's nostrils as they carried on. There was no end to the latest, most updated news on the two men who harassed the world for the last three and one-half years. Within twenty-four hours, the fear of these two prophets of God was dispelled.

Newscasts aired special features where scientific experts were brought in to testify away and explain most of what happened. A blood red moon was explained away; the heavy pollution of rice paddies being burned off sent huge smelly smoke billows into the air. Plagues were always around; they would come out when certain weather conditions were in sync. The leading world authorities of course, who were involved with the world system, explained that all was normal and safe. It was just that with the newest means of communication one could observe what a small earth they were on.

Why these things had always been going on, it's just that we could now observe them all at the same time, all over the world. Not one of them would admit that they didn't have any answers. No one dared share their individual observations. A stench of fear and death permeated the air. The truth was every plague and weather phenomena were intensifying at an alarming rate. Droughts and floods were much stronger and longer than ever recorded in history. There was a yearly increase in hurricanes and tornadoes. Weather disasters that were consistently seasonal were now year round. This caused a shortage of food and many people were starving. Of course, the news didn't show too many of these events. If world government could use it for control, showing they could give an answer, then it was televised with great joy.

Only a remnant without the mark observed the truth. "Come quickly Lord Jesus," this was the prayer of God's remaining people. They would ask for mercy and grace. By now, true believers were sincerely trying to help each other. Supporting and loving rather than allowing strife and division to trip them up. They learned to walk in unity. The church of true believers had enough of competitive religions that were full of selfish ambitions. Many in recent years were persecuted for their beliefs. Things were the same as when Jesus walked the earth. Many people were suffering and dying.

There were one hundred forty-four thousand well-meaning martyrs around the world that Jesus called home over the years. Others believers too, disappeared. The talk went around the world but soon like other times, the world leaders were quick to explain away the rapture. The most modern belief was alien or UFO abductions. Some people thought it to be true, to others a glorified hoax.

Most people though, unless they were directly involved didn't care. They were too busy making a living and keeping themselves physically fit and preparing for exotic vacations, once a year. Now that the world system was in place, people were freer to travel more than ever around the world. Since the world was cashless, all someone needed to do was walk through the proper ID check stations. Passports were no longer necessary.

By the morning of the fourth day, reporters were looking for some piece of new news. Without even trying, they got their story.

At noon, according to live witnesses in Jerusalem, the entire city grew quiet. The air was so still that one could hear his or her ears ringing. Motors of all types quit and would not start. Noisy factory machinery and hums of busy people stopped. The sky began to grow dark and mean. Angry clouds started to swirl about the atmosphere. A black fog rolled down mountainsides appearing as water cascading, falling and tripping into valleys below. Then a cold wind came in from the north until the entire sky around the world was filled with darkness. Animals started to howl as they do just before an impending storm and then grew suddenly silent again as if ordered from someone above.

Out of nowhere, in the blink of an eye, there was a flash and a cloud of bright light snapped on over the two bodies lying in the street. A gentle breeze began to blow across the corpses, ruffling their hair and lifting their clothing. "Look!" someone in the celebrating crowd shouted. "The men are breathing!"

"Nah," another answered. "The breeze just makes them look that way."

"They have been dead for three and one-half days," chimed in a third person.

But, much to everyone's amazement, the men rose. As the men were getting to their feet, a loud voice from heaven commanded them, "Come up here!" They went up to Heaven in a cloud as their enemies watched them ascend. People again, began to be filled with great fear. The light grew brighter and larger as it burned away all the darkness around. People fainted dead away at the very moment a huge earthquake hit the city. The shudder was so intense that the entire globe shook. A tenth of the city was leveled into ruins.

Seven thousand people died that day. Survivors turned to God and began giving glory to Him. Terrified, they acknowledged that Christ and not antichrist is the true Lord of all. The sky was filled with singing and beings. There were seven huge angels amongst the beings. They were carrying seven trumpets which they began to sound. A joyful and triumphant sound reverberated out of the trumpets from one end of the earth to the other.

Vapors

Susan's Story

"Okay, Gypsy, I'm awake, but I still don't want to get out from underneath this quilt. " I smiled and gave her a pat on the head. Still dark outside, I fumbled with the brass bed lamp next to me and sat up. My wolf malamute mix whined and kept at me as I pulled up my Levis and shimmied into a red turtleneck sweater. I limped toward the kitchen and warm rock fireplace. Fading embers flickered and a soft glow continued, but I struggled to put a on log on for good measure. Gypsy's cobalt eyes followed me around the room and she randomly pawed at the wooden front door. I threw on an oversized plaid coat over my shoulders and buttoned it up snug. I slipped my stocking covered feet into black ankle boots.

Canadian air blasted my face as I opened the door and stepped out onto the icy front porch. The sun sat on the edge of the horizon with ever increasing light that danced on the clouds and a fading aurora borealis. A full moon still hung in the lavender sky. The sight made revealed a worthy start to such an early day.

"Gypsy!" I hollered at her as she bounded out of sight into the surrounding fir trees. I could hear her bark at something. Afraid it could be a large animal in the area; I hollered again and sat down on our favorite large grey rock near the beach.

"Where did you go girl? You make me nervous when you do this to me and I don't know where you are." She galloped toward me and I could see something move in the trees behind. "What's that silly grin on you?" Her wiggling body language indicated she knew something. I felt nervous and wondered if I should head back.

I blinked my eyes bewildered by a vapor that moved closer. At first I thought it was part of a fog bank, but as it came closer, it grew brighter and suddenly an all but transparent form stood before me. An apparition of white appeared to be a woman, somewhat taller than me. If I believed in angels, I guessed that could be this. I shivered, but felt sense of calm serenity wash over me.

She spoke. "Don't be afraid Susan. I'm here to help, not harm."

I believed her, Gypsy behaved in an unusual manner. She wagged her tail and hunched by my side. Most of the time, she won't let anyone near me.

"Listen to me sweet girl, have you wondered the reason that you are living? People live to help others in good times and bad times. I know you've been so sick and you've wanted to give up. The truth is that everyone is dying from the day they are born. I know your pain and you wonder if this will ever cease." She grew silent and her intense eyes bored deep into my very soul. I couldn't take my eyes off this magnificent beauty; her voice compelled my attention.

"Susan, you're coming close to the end, there is no denying it and you know it too, but you wonder how you've survived this long. Life hasn't been kind, you've been near the edge many times, yet you've not given up. You've determinedly hung onto life, and been given many chances. I know you are so tired, my dear." She sighed and touched me ever so slightly with a brush of her hand. She quivered and I felt warmth and love, indescribable as I accepted the deepest form of love from her touch.

I summoned up courage, "Who…um who are you? I didn't want to run from her, I wanted another touch, a stroke of a wing feather perhaps, but this being didn't have wings. She looked like any other human, except light permeated her entire being.

"I'm your guardian angel, Susan; I've been assigned to you since the moment you were born. I know you don't believe in such things, we have never left you, just waited for you to come. You've beat the odds in your life several times, remember the ski accident, and mis-carriages, and then there was that medical mess-up with your medications, not to mention all the surgeries. All that time, you remained a trooper and encouraged others in your life."

"Who are we? There's only one of you here." I glanced around for more forms. *I often wondered how I'd made it this long.*

The angel spoke, "Why Jesus of course, he's with you the moment you invite him into your heart." She laughed and continued, "Yes, we have wings occasionally if necessary."

I gasped, "How did you know what I was thinking?"

"Because the Father knows everything"

I could feel my eyebrows raise together, "Father?"

"Susan, our father is God, Father of Jesus Christ; he was born to die and to rise on the third day so that we could enjoy heaven with him and our Father. He died on a cross for your sin and rose on the third day, just as the scriptures are written. God, the Father gives each person a chance to repent and come to Jesus and accept him as their personal savior. We identify with him as we live on earth. Every person is a born sinner, born into a sinful world. Every sinner must learn and realize this and repent of his or her sins, known and unknown."

I said, "A couple of people over the years shared that with me, but I didn't believe such fairy tales."

"Life is but a Vapor Susan. You are almost done on earth, but there's one unfinished business and Jesus sent me to help." She touched me again. "Yes, I know you aren't a believer but I'm here, your guardian angel to ask you to forgive all the hurts thrust upon you by others, to recognize that you are a sinner and ask forgiveness of all your rebellion, and acknowledge Jesus Christ, accepting him as your personal savior."

"I don't understand everything but it seems much clearer to me now. Please pray with me to accept the truth and Jesus." I bowed my head and reached out to this being, which I now believed, was an angel.

She led me through the sinner's prayer and told me of the many people that prayed for me over the years. I can't describe the experience of cleanliness, inside and out that filled me. Overjoyed I reached my arms upward, my eyes were closed.

"Let's meet Jesus precious child." The angel whispered.

My body seemed lighter, like somehow I changed. I opened my eyes and to my dismay, my spirit floated above the ground.

I saw a limp body, mine, on the rock and I told Gypsy to run back to the house. She obeyed me with one long howl, the wolf telling me goodbye. "I love you Gypsy, thank you for being my faithful companion."

Revelation

11:14, 15, 16,17,18,19 Taken from the <u>King James Bible</u>

14 "The second woe is past; and behold, the third woe cometh quickly.

And the seventh angel sounded; and there were great voices in heaven saying,

15   The kingdoms of this world are becoming the kingdoms of our Lord, and of his Christ; and he shall reign forever and ever. Isaiah 27:134

16 And the four and twenty elders, which sat before God on their seats, fell upon their faces and

Worshiped God,

17 Saying,

We give thee thanks, Oh Lord God Almighty, which art, and wast, and art to come; because

Thou hast taken to thee thy great power, and hast reigned.

18 And the nations were angry, and thy wrath is come, and the time of the dead, that they should

be judged, and that thou shouldest give reward unto thy servants the prophets, land to the

Saints and them that fear thy name, small and great: and shouldest destroy them which destroy the earth.

19 And, the temple of God was opened in heaven, and there was seen in His temple the ark of

His testament: and there was lightening, and voices, and thundering, and an earthquake, and real hail.

Revelation 8: The Seventh Trumpet taken from <u>The Message-Navpress</u>

Blowing the Trumpets

I saw the Seven Angels who are always in readiness before God handed seven trumpets.

Then another Angel, carrying a gold censer, came and stood at the Altar. He was given a great quantity of incense so that he could offer up the prayers of all the holy people of God on the Golden Altar before the Throne. Smoke billowed up from the incense-laced prayers of the holy ones, rose before God from the hand of the Angel.

Then the Angel filled the censer with fire from the Altar and heaved it to the earth. It set off thunders, voices, lightening, and an earthquake.

The Seven Angels with the trumpets got ready to blow them. At the first trumpet blast, hail and fire mixed with blood were dumped on earth. A third of the earth was scorched, a third of the trees and every blade of green grass burned to a crisp.

The second Angel trumpeted. Something like a huge mountain blazing with fire was flung into the sea. A third of the sea turned to blood, a third of the living sea creatures died, and a third of the ships sank.

The third Angel trumpeted. A huge Star, blazing like a torch, fell from Heaven, wiping out a third of the rivers and a third of the springs.

The Stars; name was Wormwood. A third of the water turned bitter, and many people died from the poisoned water.

The fourth Angel trumpeted. A third of the sun, a third of the moon, and a third of the stars were hit, blacked out by a third, both day and night in one-third blackout.

I looked hard; I heard a lone eagle, flying through Middle heaven, crying out ominously, "Doom! Doom! Doom! To everyone left on earth! There are three more Angels about to blow their trumpets. Doom is on its way!"

Revelation 9

The fifth Angel trumpeted. I saw a Star plummet from Heaven to earth. The Star was handed a key to the Well of the Abyss. He unlocked the Well of the Abyss----Smoke poured out of the Well, billows and billows of smoke, sun and air in blackout from smoke pouring out of the Well.

Then out of the smoke crawled locusts with the venom of scorpions. They were given their orders: "Don't hurt the grass, don't hurt anything green, don't hurt a single tree---only men and women, and then only those who lack the seal of God on their foreheads." They were ordered to torture but not to kill, torture them for five months, the pain like a scorpion sting.

When this happens, people are going to prefer death to torture, look for ways to kill themselves.

But they won't find a way---death will have gone into hiding.

The locusts looked like horses ready for war. They had gold crowns, human faces, women's hair, the teeth of lions, and iron breastplates. The sound of their wings was the sound of horse-drawn chariots charging into battle. Their tails were equipped with stings, like scorpion tails. With those tails they were ordered to torture the human race for five months. They had a king over them, the Angel of the Abyss. His name in Hebrew is Abaddon, in Greek, Apollyon---"Destroyer."

The first doom is past. Two dooms yet to come.

The sixth Angel trumpeted.

I heard a voice speaking to the sixth Angel from the horns

of the Golden Altar before God: "Let the Four Angels loose, the Angels confined at the great River Euphrates."

The Four Angels were untied and let loose, Four Angels all prepared for the exact year, month, day, and even hour when they were to kill a third of the human race. The number of the army of horsemen was twice ten thousand times ten thousand. I heard the count and saw both horses and riders in my vision: fiery breastplates on the riders, lion heads on the horses breathing out fire and smoke and brimstone. With these three weapons---fire and smoke and brimstone--they killed a third of the human race. The horses killed them with their mouths and tails; their serpent-like tails also had heads that wreaked havoc.

The remaining men and women who weren't killed by these weapons went on their merry way---didn't change their way of life, didn't quit worshiping demons, didn't quit centering their lives around lumps of gold and silver and brass, hunks of stone and wood that couldn't see or hear or move. There wasn't a sign of a change of heart. They plunged right on in their murderous, occult, promiscuous, and thieving ways.

Revelation 10

I saw another powerful Angel coming down out of Heaven wrapped in a cloud. There was a rainbow over his head, his face was sun-radiant, his legs pillars of fire. He had a small book open in his hand. He placed his right foot on land, and then called out thunderously, a lion roar. When he called out, the Seven Thunders called back. When the Seven Thunders spoke, I started to write it all down, but a voice out of Heaven stopped me, saying, "Seal with silence the Seven Thunders; don't write a word."

Then the Angel I saw astride sea and land lifted his right hand to Heaven and swore by the One Living Forever and Ever, who Created Heaven and everything in it, earth and everything in it, sea and everything in it, that time was up---that when the Seventh Angel blew his trumpet, which he was about to do, the

Mystery of God, all the plans he had revealed to his servants, the prophets, would be completed.

The voice out of Heaven spoke to me again: "Go, take the book held open in the hand of the Angel astride sea and earth." I went up to the Angel and said, "Give me the little book." He said, "Take it, then eat it. It will taste sweet like honey, but it will turn sour in your stomach." I took the little book from the Angels' hand and it was sweet honey in my mouth, but when I swallowed, my stomach curdled. Then I was told, "You must go back and prophesy again over many peoples and nations and languages and kings.

Revelation 11
The Two Witnesses

I was given a stick for a measuring rod and told, "Get up and measure Gods' Temple and Altar and everyone worshiping in it. Exclude the outside court; don't measure it. It's been handed over to non-Jewish outsiders. They desecrated the Holy City for forty-two months.

"Meanwhile, I'll provide my two Witnesses. Dressed in sackcloth, they'll prophesy for one thousand two hundred sixty days. These are the two Olive Trees, the two Lamp stands, standing at attention before God on earth. If anyone tries to hurt them, a blast of fire from their mouths will incinerate them---burn them to a crisp just like that. They'll have power to seal the sky so that it doesn't rain for the time of their prophesying, power to turn rivers and springs to blood, power to hit earth with any and every disaster as often as they want.

"When they've completed their witness, the Beast from the Abyss will emerge and fight them, conquer and kill them, leaving their corpses exposed on the street of the Great City spiritually called Sodom and Egypt, the same City where their Master was crucified. For three and a half days they'll be there ---exposed, prevented from getting a decent burial, stared at by the curious from all over the world. Those people will cheer at the spectacle, shouting "Good riddance!" and calling for a celebration, for these two prophets pricked the conscience of all the people on earth, made it impossible for them to enjoy their sins.

"Then, after three and half days, the Living Spirit of God will enter them---they're on their feet!---and all those gloating spectators will be scared to death."

I heard a strong voice out of Heaven calling "Come up here!" and up they went to Heaven; wrapped in a cloud, their enemies watching it all. At that moment there was a gigantic earthquake---a tenth of the City fell to ruin, seven thousand perished in the earthquake, the rest frightened into giving honor to the God of Heaven.

The second doom is past, the third doom coming right on its heels.

THE LAST TRUMPET SOUNDS

The Seventh Angel trumpeted. A crescendo of voices in Heaven sang out,

"The kingdom of the world is now the Kingdom of our God and his Messiah! He will rule forever and ever!" The Twenty-four Elders seated before God on their thrones fell to their knees, worshiped and sang, "We thank you, Oh God, Sovereign-Strong,

WHO IS AND WHO WAS

You took your great power and took over-reigned! The angry nations now get a taste of your anger. The time has come to judge the dead, to reward your servants, all prophets and saints, Reward small and great who fear your name, and destroy the destroyers of earth."

The doors of Gods' Temple in Heaven flew open, and the Ark of his Covenant was clearly seen surrounded by flashes of lightning, loud shouts, peals of thunder, an earthquake, and a fierce hailstorm.

All now listen…listen to the sounding of God's trumpets

and realize that the Savior draws near to you. The Seventh Angel is blowing the **Seventh Trumpet!**
    Amen and
    Amen it is finished.

A Word of Love to My Fellow Soldiers

Dear reader,

God in His infinite love for the human creature does not will for anyone to miss out on His wonderful blessings. He calls each one to His body to be held and loved. I am aware of pre-trib, post-trib, and many other interpretations of the Bible. The point of this book is to focus on our Lord Jesus Christ and what He has to say right now in this period of our History. Don't worry about these things; let the world debate as they always have. **This story is purely fictional and speculative. This pertains to no known persons, but humanity as a whole.**

Too many well-meaning people in this time of History do not pick up the Bible and look for the answers themselves. There are many good Christian denominations in the world today. Being a part of the body of Christ is only a small piece of having His fullness in your life. Too many depend on others for spiritual food.

Fellow Christians, it's time to feed yourselves, you have lived on milk long enough. Pick up your mat of dependence on others and fill yourselves with His Holy Word, that you may follow Him as He directs your path. Fill yourselves that you may be a blessing to others and love them along their way. For, the Word tells us "the road is narrow and there are many false paths and stumbling blocks."

Be free in Christ, that you may free others. No more, be critical and divisive of one another lest you be devoured yourselves. False leaders and wolves in sheep's clothing will multiply within the body of Christ. God will show you. Stay away from anything or anyone that does not point to Christ or is producing bad fruit. The times are perilous my brothers and sisters, pray constantly for one another.

God has given us countless warnings throughout the ages, doubtless, He will continue but look for yourselves! Are not the signs and wonders all around us?! Cheer up! Get your eyes upon Jesus!!!!

                                    Love,
                                    Paulette, your sister in Christ Jesus

May God's love bless your life!

Made in the USA
Columbia, SC
24 June 2020